DEAD SAMURAI
死侍

BY ARON LUSEN

A Komikwerks Production
Published by ibooks, inc.

ibooks

KOMIKWERKS

GN
Lusen
V.1

DEAD SAMURAI, Vol. 1.
NOVEMBER 2005.

PUBLISHED BY IBOOKS, INC.
24 West 25 STREET
NEW YORK, NY 10010

PUBLISHED IN ASSOCIATION WITH KOMIKWERKS, LLC.
WWW.KOMIKWERKS.COM

EBOOK VERSION AVAILABLE THROUGH WWW.KOMIKWERKS.COM.

10 9 8 7 6 5 4 3 2 1
ISBN: 1-59687-828-2

DISTRIBUTED IN THE UNITED STATES AND CANADA BY
PUBLISHERS GROUP WEST

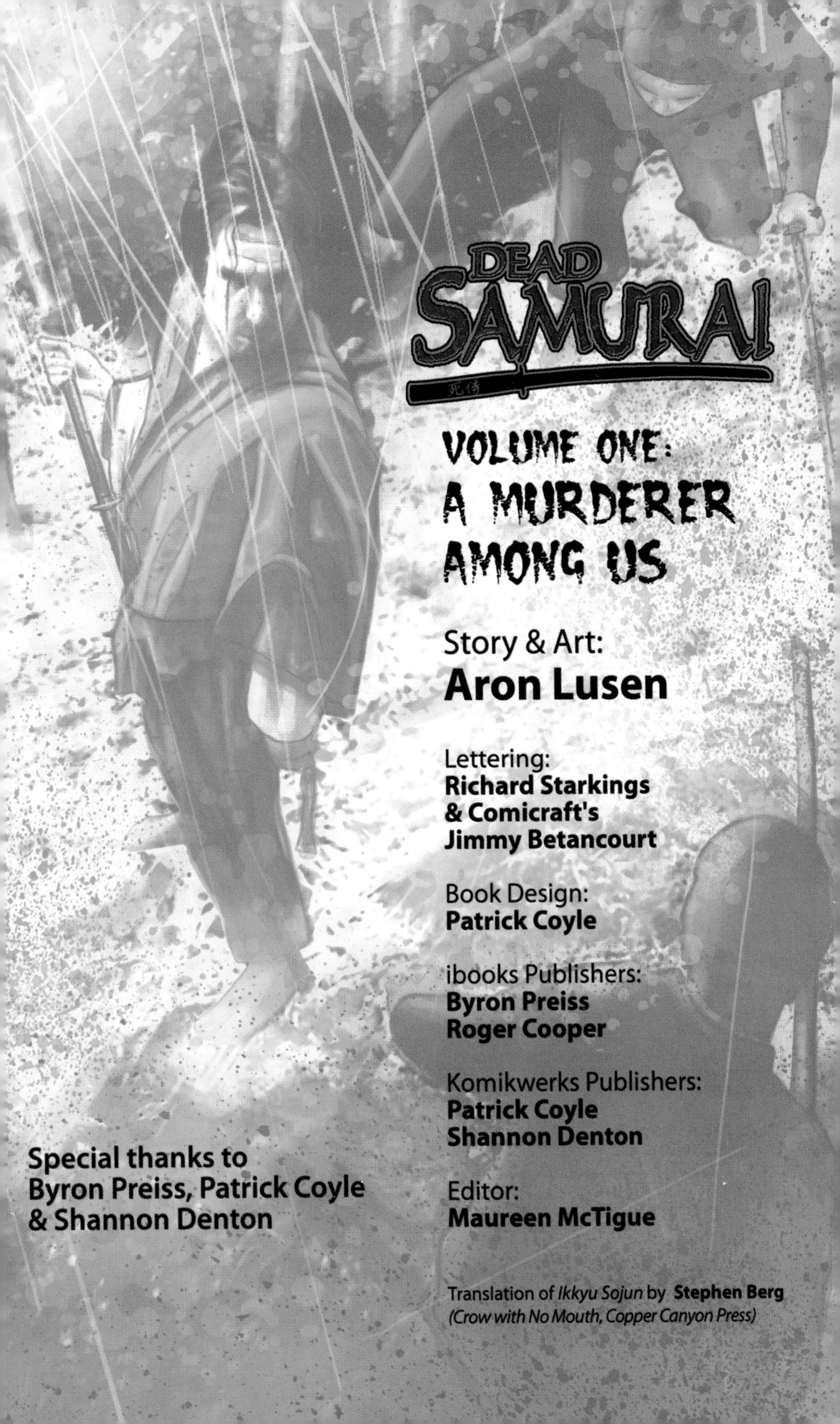

DEAD SAMURAI

VOLUME ONE: A MURDERER AMONG US

Story & Art:
Aron Lusen

Lettering:
Richard Starkings & Comicraft's Jimmy Betancourt

Book Design:
Patrick Coyle

ibooks Publishers:
Byron Preiss
Roger Cooper

Komikwerks Publishers:
Patrick Coyle
Shannon Denton

Editor:
Maureen McTigue

Special thanks to Byron Preiss, Patrick Coyle & Shannon Denton

Translation of *Ikkyu Sojun* by **Stephen Berg**
(Crow with No Mouth, Copper Canyon Press)

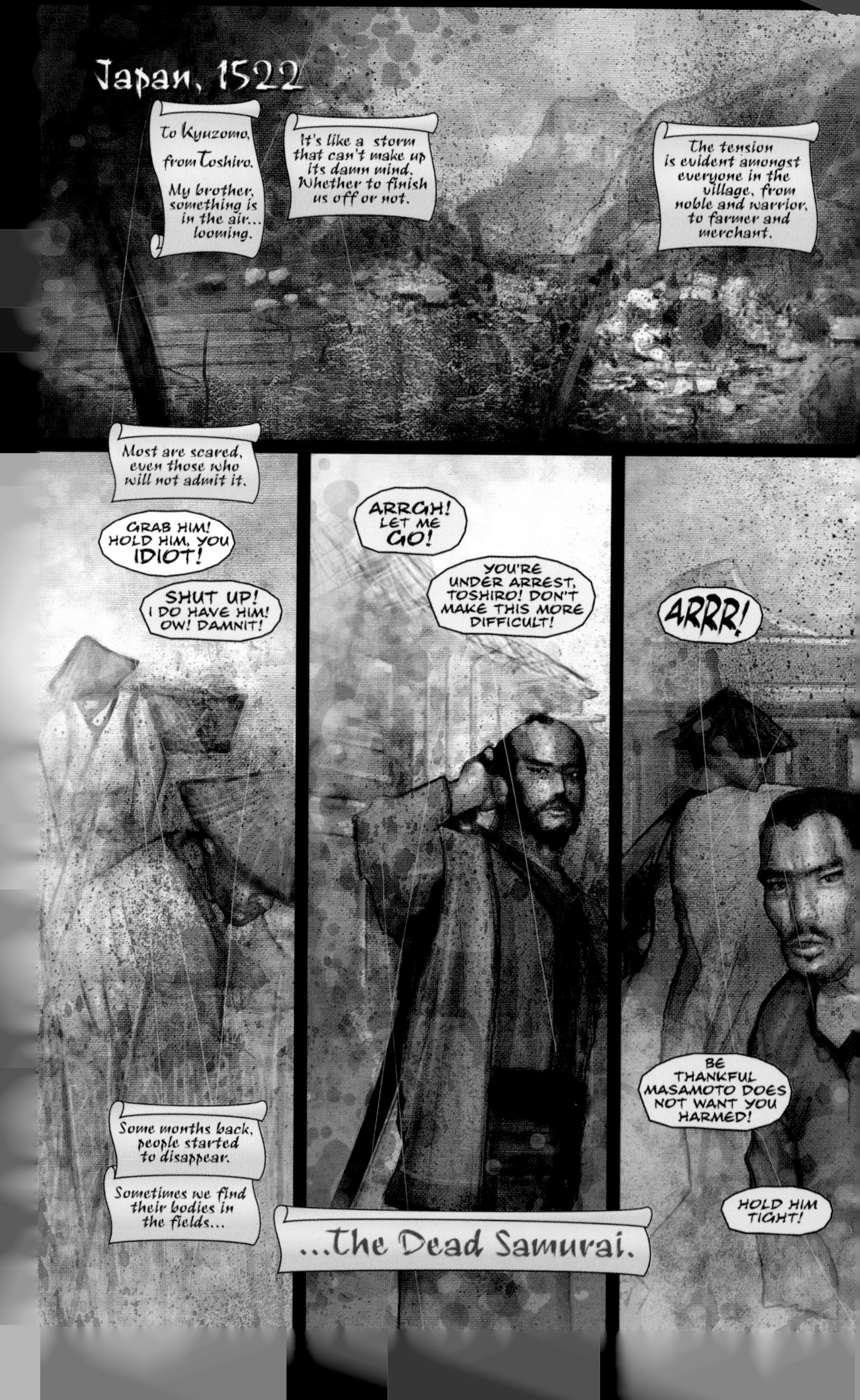
Japan, 1522
To Kyuzomo, from Toshiro. My brother, something is in the air... looming.
It's like a storm that can't make up its damn mind. Whether to finish us off or not.
The tension is evident amongst everyone in the village, from noble and warrior, to farmer and merchant.
Most are scared, even those who will not admit it.
GRAB HIM! HOLD HIM, YOU IDIOT!
SHUT UP! I DO HAVE HIM! OW! DAMNIT!
ARRGH! LET ME GO!
YOU'RE UNDER ARREST, TOSHIRO! DON'T MAKE THIS MORE DIFFICULT!
ARRR!
BE THANKFUL MASAMOTO DOES NOT WANT YOU HARMED!
HOLD HIM TIGHT!
Some months back, people started to disappear.
Sometimes we find their bodies in the fields...
...The Dead Samurai.

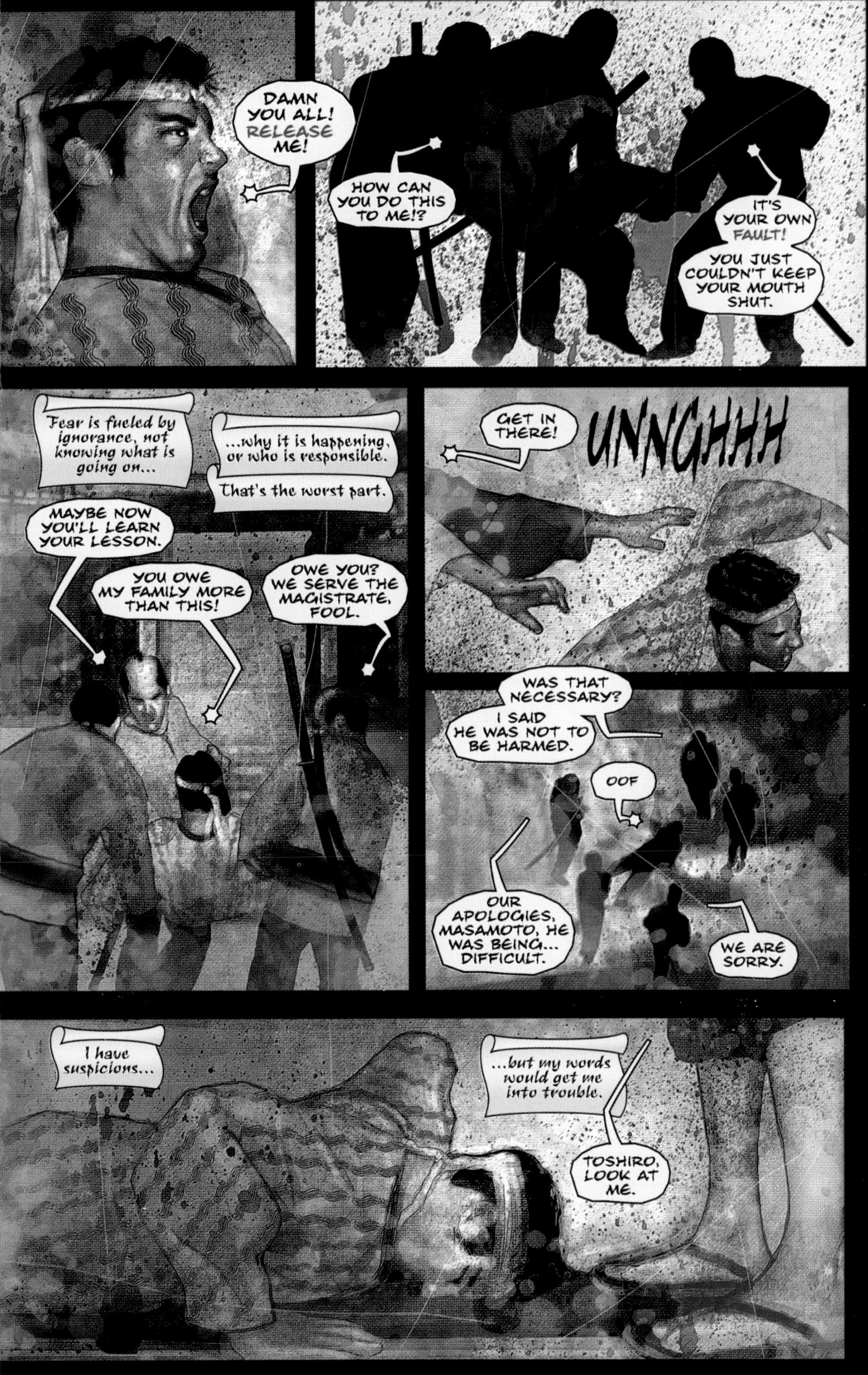
DAMN YOU ALL! RELEASE ME!
HOW CAN YOU DO THIS TO ME!?
IT'S YOUR OWN FAULT!
YOU JUST COULDN'T KEEP YOUR MOUTH SHUT.
Fear is fueled by ignorance, not knowing what is going on...
...why it is happening, or who is responsible.
That's the worst part.
MAYBE NOW YOU'LL LEARN YOUR LESSON.
YOU OWE MY FAMILY MORE THAN THIS!
OWE YOU? WE SERVE THE MAGISTRATE, FOOL.
GET IN THERE!
UNNGHHH
WAS THAT NECESSARY?
I SAID HE WAS NOT TO BE HARMED.
OOF
OUR APOLOGIES, MASAMOTO, HE WAS BEING... DIFFICULT.
WE ARE SORRY.
I have suspicions...
...but my words would get me into trouble.
TOSHIRO, LOOK AT ME.

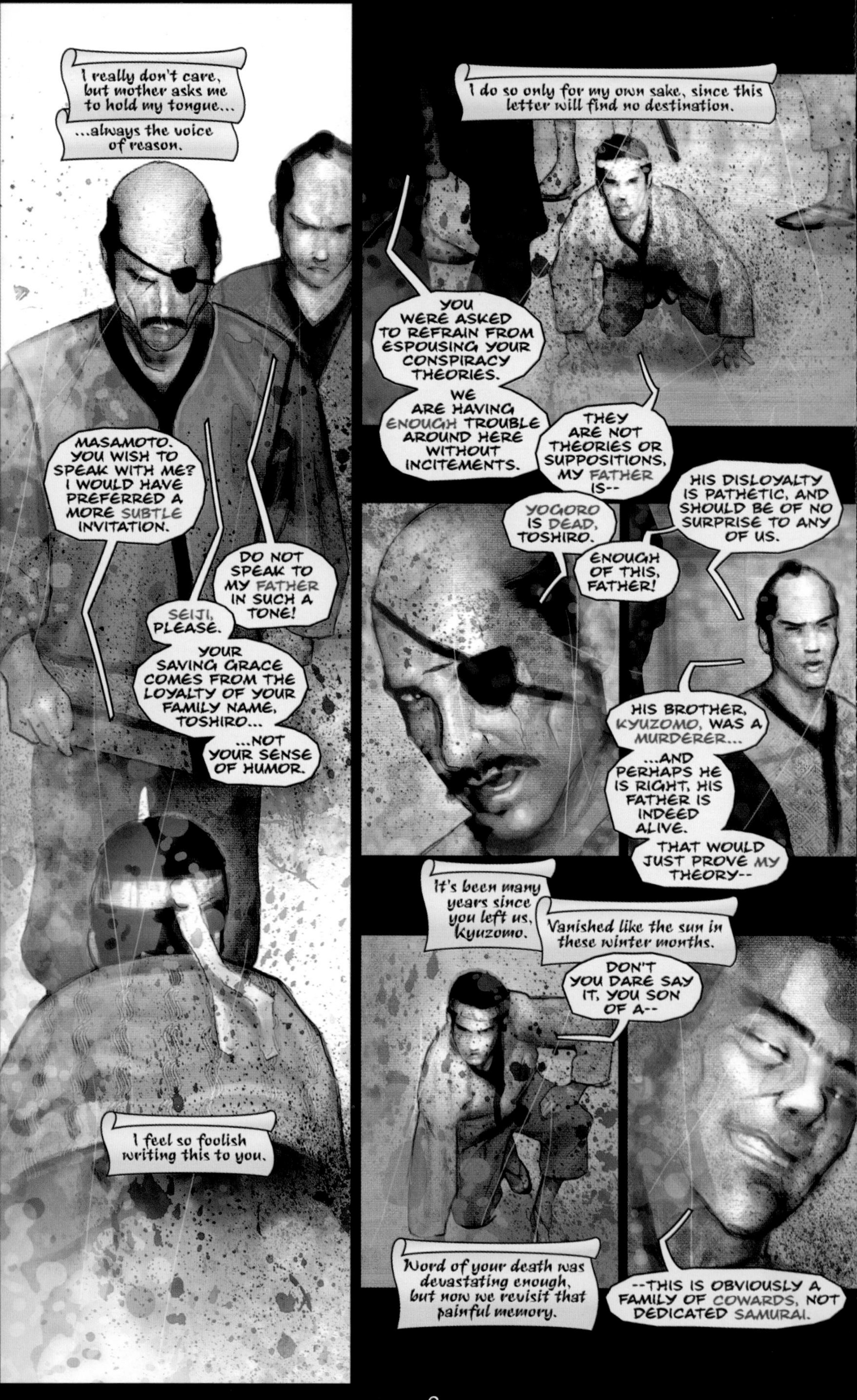
I really don't care, but mother asks me to hold my tongue...
...always the voice of reason.
MASAMOTO. YOU WISH TO SPEAK WITH ME? I WOULD HAVE PREFERRED A MORE SUBTLE INVITATION.
DO NOT SPEAK TO MY FATHER IN SUCH A TONE!
SEIJI, PLEASE.
YOUR SAVING GRACE COMES FROM THE LOYALTY OF YOUR FAMILY NAME, TOSHIRO...
...NOT YOUR SENSE OF HUMOR.
I feel so foolish writing this to you.
I do so only for my own sake, since this letter will find no destination.
YOU WERE ASKED TO REFRAIN FROM ESPOUSING YOUR CONSPIRACY THEORIES.
WE ARE HAVING ENOUGH TROUBLE AROUND HERE WITHOUT INCITEMENTS.
THEY ARE NOT THEORIES OR SUPPOSITIONS, MY FATHER IS--
YOGORO IS DEAD, TOSHIRO.
ENOUGH OF THIS, FATHER!
HIS DISLOYALTY IS PATHETIC, AND SHOULD BE OF NO SURPRISE TO ANY OF US.
HIS BROTHER, KYUZOMO, WAS A MURDERER...
...AND PERHAPS HE IS RIGHT, HIS FATHER IS INDEED ALIVE.
THAT WOULD JUST PROVE MY THEORY--
It's been many years since you left us, Kyuzomo.
Vanished like the sun in these winter months.
DON'T YOU DARE SAY IT, YOU SON OF A--
Word of your death was devastating enough, but now we revisit that painful memory.
--THIS IS OBVIOUSLY A FAMILY OF COWARDS, NOT DEDICATED SAMURAI.

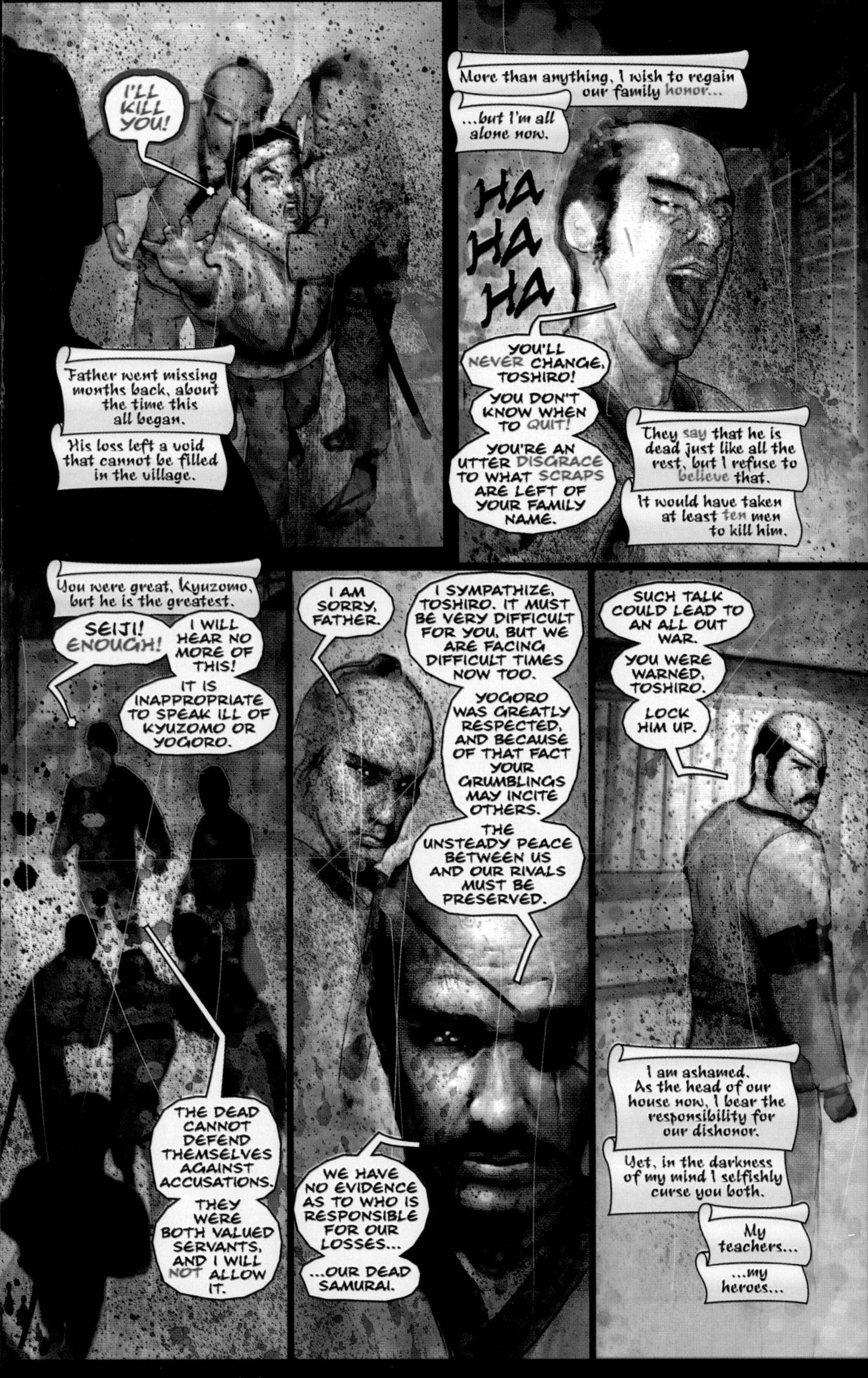
I'LL KILL YOU!
Father went missing months back, about the time this all began.
His loss left a void that cannot be filled in the village.
More than anything, I wish to regain our family honor...
...but I'm all alone now.
HA HA HA
YOU'LL NEVER CHANGE, TOSHIRO!
YOU DON'T KNOW WHEN TO QUIT!
YOU'RE AN UTTER DISGRACE TO WHAT SCRAPS ARE LEFT OF YOUR FAMILY NAME.
They say that he is dead just like all the rest, but I refuse to believe that.
It would have taken at least ten men to kill him.
You were great, Kyuzomo, but he is the greatest.
SEIJI! ENOUGH!
I WILL HEAR NO MORE OF THIS!
IT IS INAPPROPRIATE TO SPEAK ILL OF KYUZOMO OR YOGORO.
THE DEAD CANNOT DEFEND THEMSELVES AGAINST ACCUSATIONS.
THEY WERE BOTH VALUED SERVANTS, AND I WILL NOT ALLOW IT.
I AM SORRY, FATHER.
I SYMPATHIZE, TOSHIRO. IT MUST BE VERY DIFFICULT FOR YOU, BUT WE ARE FACING DIFFICULT TIMES NOW TOO.
YOGORO WAS GREATLY RESPECTED, AND BECAUSE OF THAT FACT YOUR GRUMBLINGS MAY INCITE OTHERS.
THE UNSTEADY PEACE BETWEEN US AND OUR RIVALS MUST BE PRESERVED.
WE HAVE NO EVIDENCE AS TO WHO IS RESPONSIBLE FOR OUR LOSSES...
...OUR DEAD SAMURAI.
SUCH TALK COULD LEAD TO AN ALL OUT WAR.
YOU WERE WARNED, TOSHIRO.
LOCK HIM UP.
I am ashamed. As the head of our house now, I bear the responsibility for our dishonor.
Yet, in the darkness of my mind I selfishly curse you both.
My teachers...
...my heroes...

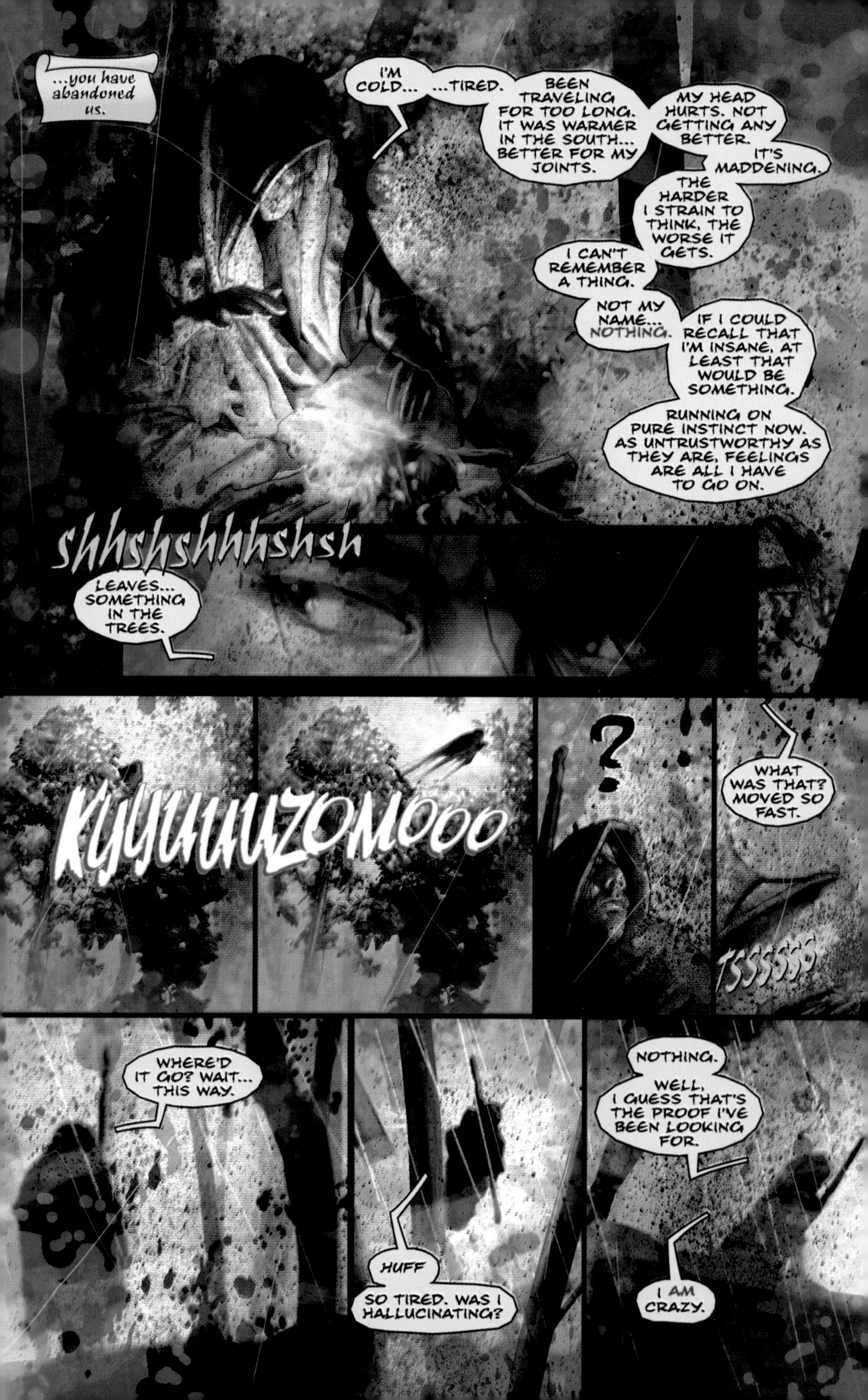
...you have abandoned us.
I'M COLD... ...TIRED.
BEEN TRAVELING FOR TOO LONG. IT WAS WARMER IN THE SOUTH... BETTER FOR MY JOINTS.
MY HEAD HURTS. NOT GETTING ANY BETTER.
IT'S MADDENING.
THE HARDER I STRAIN TO THINK, THE WORSE IT GETS.
I CAN'T REMEMBER A THING.
NOT MY NAME... NOTHING.
IF I COULD RECALL THAT I'M INSANE, AT LEAST THAT WOULD BE SOMETHING.
RUNNING ON PURE INSTINCT NOW. AS UNTRUSTWORTHY AS THEY ARE, FEELINGS ARE ALL I HAVE TO GO ON.
shhshshhhshsh
LEAVES... SOMETHING IN THE TREES.
KYUUUUZOMOOO
?
WHAT WAS THAT? MOVED SO FAST.
TSSSSSS
WHERE'D IT GO? WAIT... THIS WAY.
HUFF
SO TIRED. WAS I HALLUCINATING?
NOTHING.
WELL, I GUESS THAT'S THE PROOF I'VE BEEN LOOKING FOR.
I AM CRAZY.

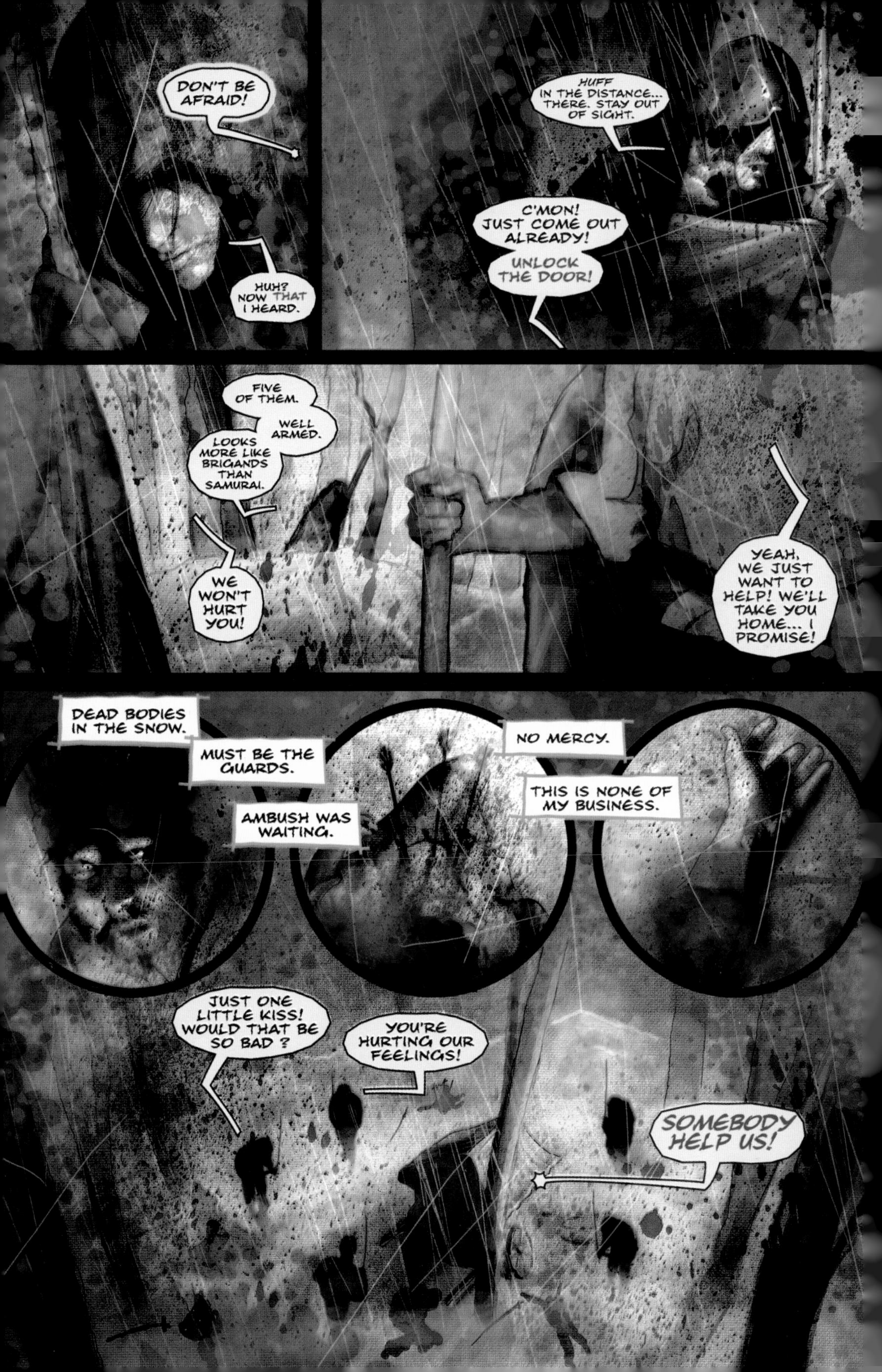
DON'T BE AFRAID!
HUH? NOW THAT I HEARD.
HUFF IN THE DISTANCE... THERE. STAY OUT OF SIGHT.
C'MON! JUST COME OUT ALREADY!
UNLOCK THE DOOR!
FIVE OF THEM.
WELL ARMED.
LOOKS MORE LIKE BRIGANDS THAN SAMURAI.
WE WON'T HURT YOU!
YEAH, WE JUST WANT TO HELP! WE'LL TAKE YOU HOME... I PROMISE!
DEAD BODIES IN THE SNOW.
MUST BE THE GUARDS.
AMBUSH WAS WAITING.
NO MERCY.
THIS IS NONE OF MY BUSINESS.
JUST ONE LITTLE KISS! WOULD THAT BE SO BAD ?
YOU'RE HURTING OUR FEELINGS!
SOMEBODY HELP US!

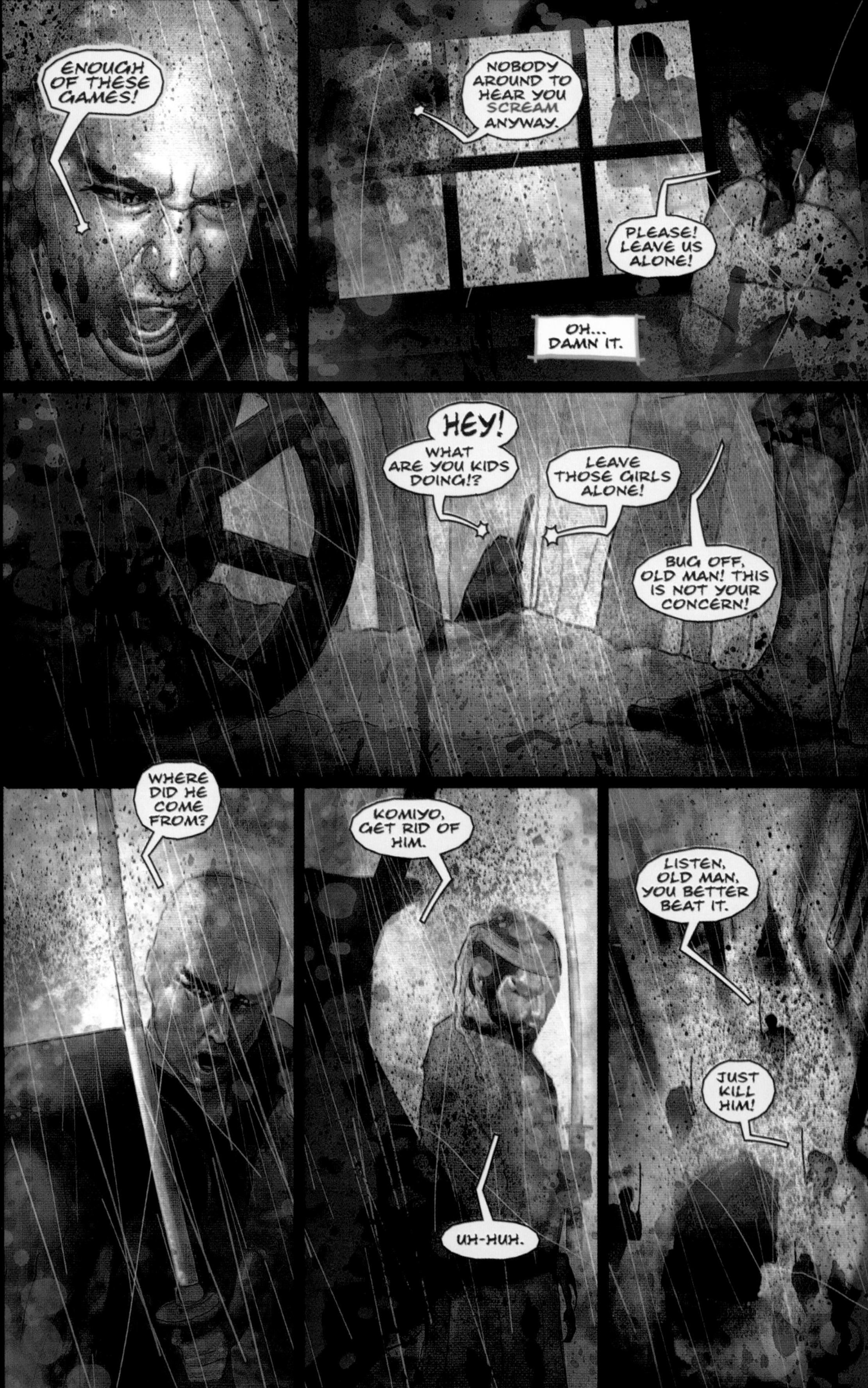
ENOUGH OF THESE GAMES!
NOBODY AROUND TO HEAR YOU SCREAM ANYWAY.
PLEASE! LEAVE US ALONE!
OH... DAMN IT.
HEY! WHAT ARE YOU KIDS DOING!?
LEAVE THOSE GIRLS ALONE!
BUG OFF, OLD MAN! THIS IS NOT YOUR CONCERN!
WHERE DID HE COME FROM?
KOMIYO, GET RID OF HIM.
UH-HUH.
LISTEN, OLD MAN, YOU BETTER BEAT IT.
JUST KILL HIM!

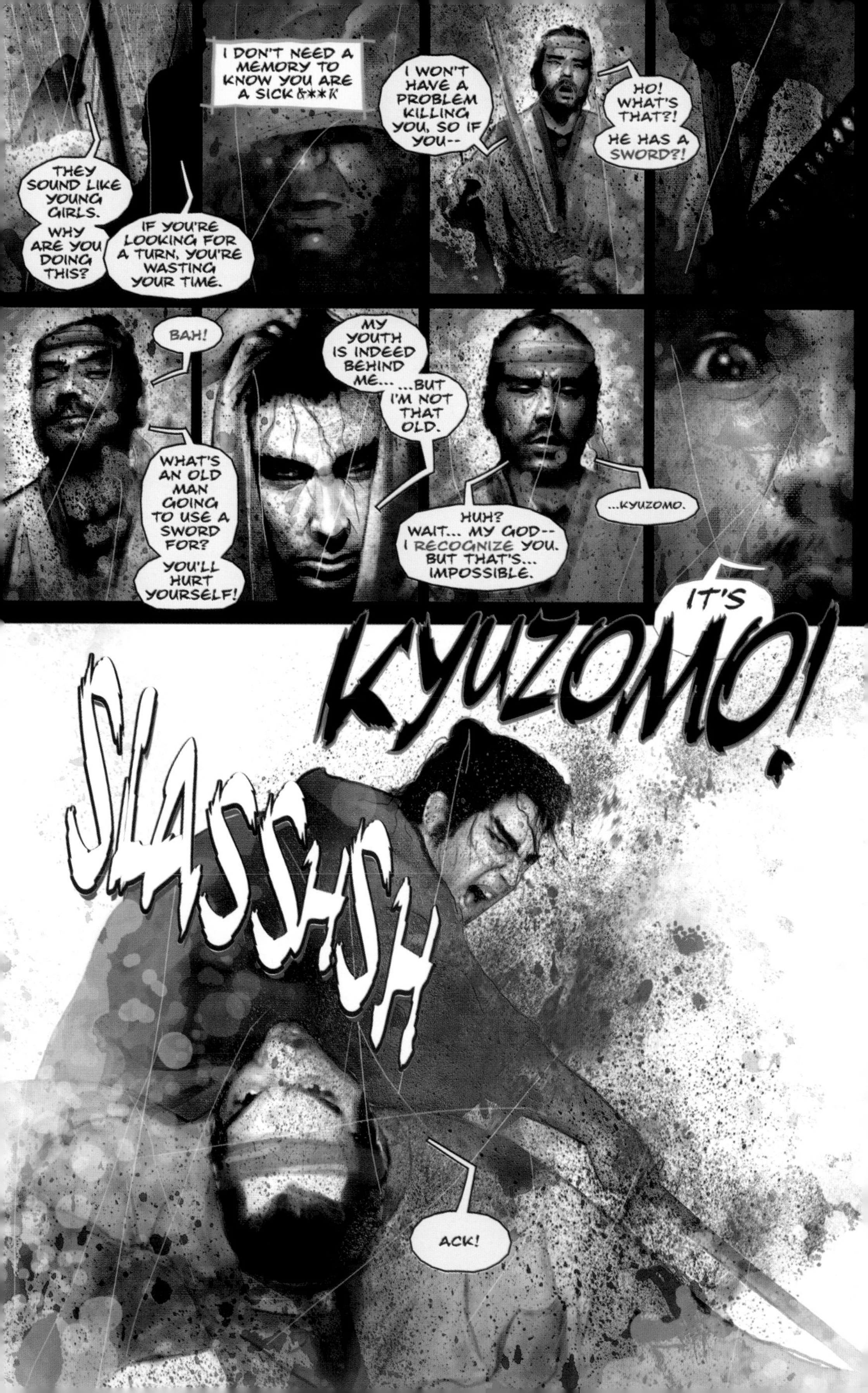
THEY SOUND LIKE YOUNG GIRLS.
WHY ARE YOU DOING THIS?
IF YOU'RE LOOKING FOR A TURN, YOU'RE WASTING YOUR TIME.
I DON'T NEED A MEMORY TO KNOW YOU ARE A SICK &**K
I WON'T HAVE A PROBLEM KILLING YOU, SO IF YOU--
HO! WHAT'S THAT?!
HE HAS A SWORD?!
BAH!
WHAT'S AN OLD MAN GOING TO USE A SWORD FOR?
YOU'LL HURT YOURSELF!
MY YOUTH IS INDEED BEHIND ME... ...BUT I'M NOT THAT OLD.
HUH? WAIT... MY GOD-- I RECOGNIZE YOU. BUT THAT'S... IMPOSSIBLE.
...KYUZOMO.
IT'S KYUZOMO!
SLASSHSH
ACK!

KILL HIM! IF THAT REALLY IS KYUZOMO, THERE IS STILL A BOUNTY!

MAYBE I AM WHO THEY SAY...

I DON'T KNOW.

BUT I SUDDENLY FEEL A PIT IN MY STOMACH.

NOT FEAR, BUT A SENSE THAT DESPITE AN AVERSION TO VIOLENCE...

...DEATH IS COMING.

IT DOESN'T MATTER NOW.

INSTINCT TAKES OVER...

...AND THE ONE THING THAT I DO SEEM TO REMEMBER...

...IS HOW TO KILL.

HACK

SLICE

GOOSH

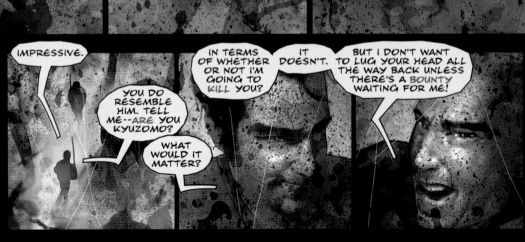

IMPRESSIVE.

YOU DO RESEMBLE HIM. TELL ME--ARE YOU KYUZOMO?

WHAT WOULD IT MATTER?

IN TERMS OF WHETHER OR NOT I'M GOING TO KILL YOU?

IT DOESN'T.

BUT I DON'T WANT TO LUG YOUR HEAD ALL THE WAY BACK UNLESS THERE'S A BOUNTY WAITING FOR ME!

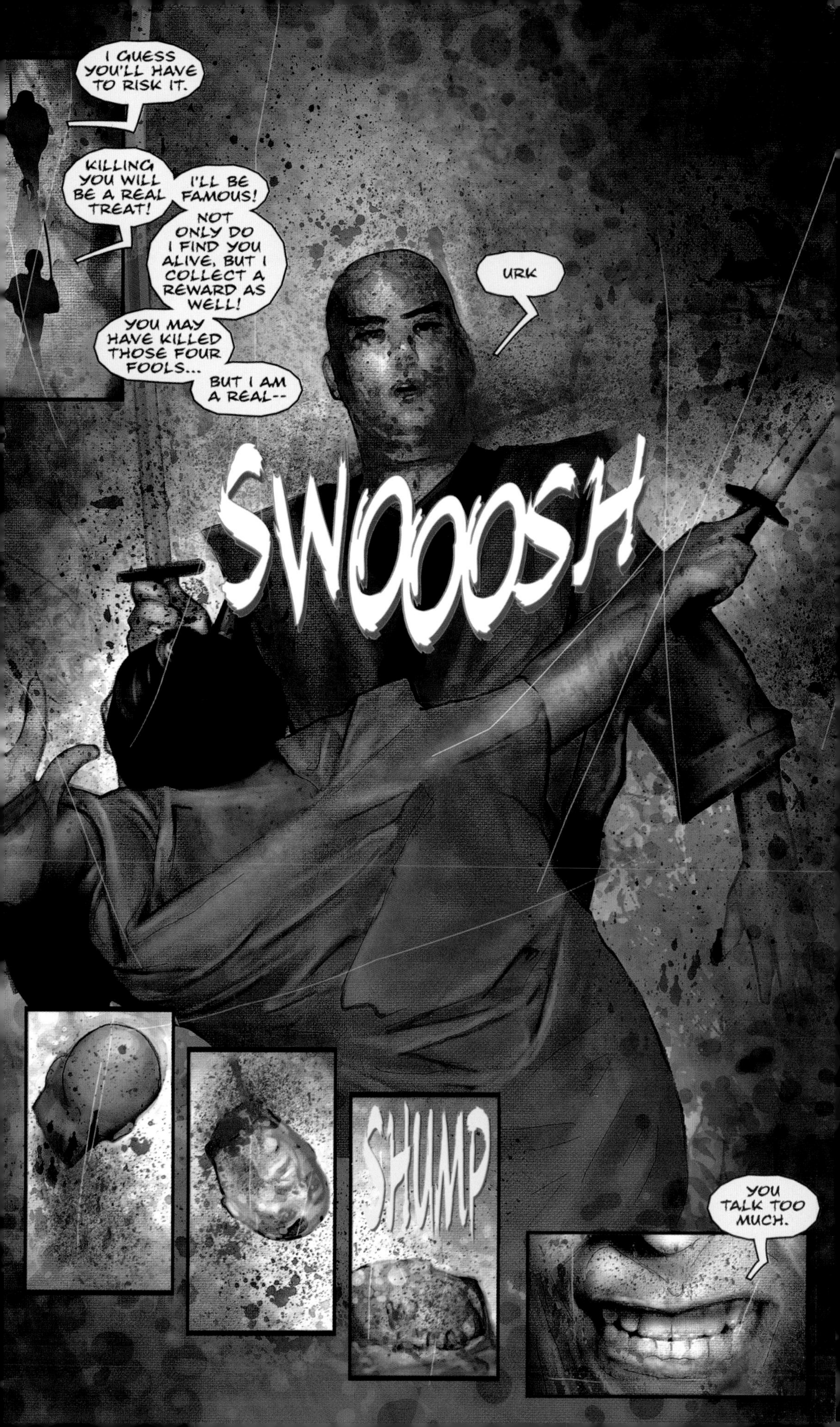
I GUESS YOU'LL HAVE TO RISK IT.
KILLING YOU WILL BE A REAL TREAT!
I'LL BE FAMOUS!
NOT ONLY DO I FIND YOU ALIVE, BUT I COLLECT A REWARD AS WELL!
YOU MAY HAVE KILLED THOSE FOUR FOOLS...
BUT I AM A REAL--
URK
SWOOOSH
SHUMP
YOU TALK TOO MUCH.

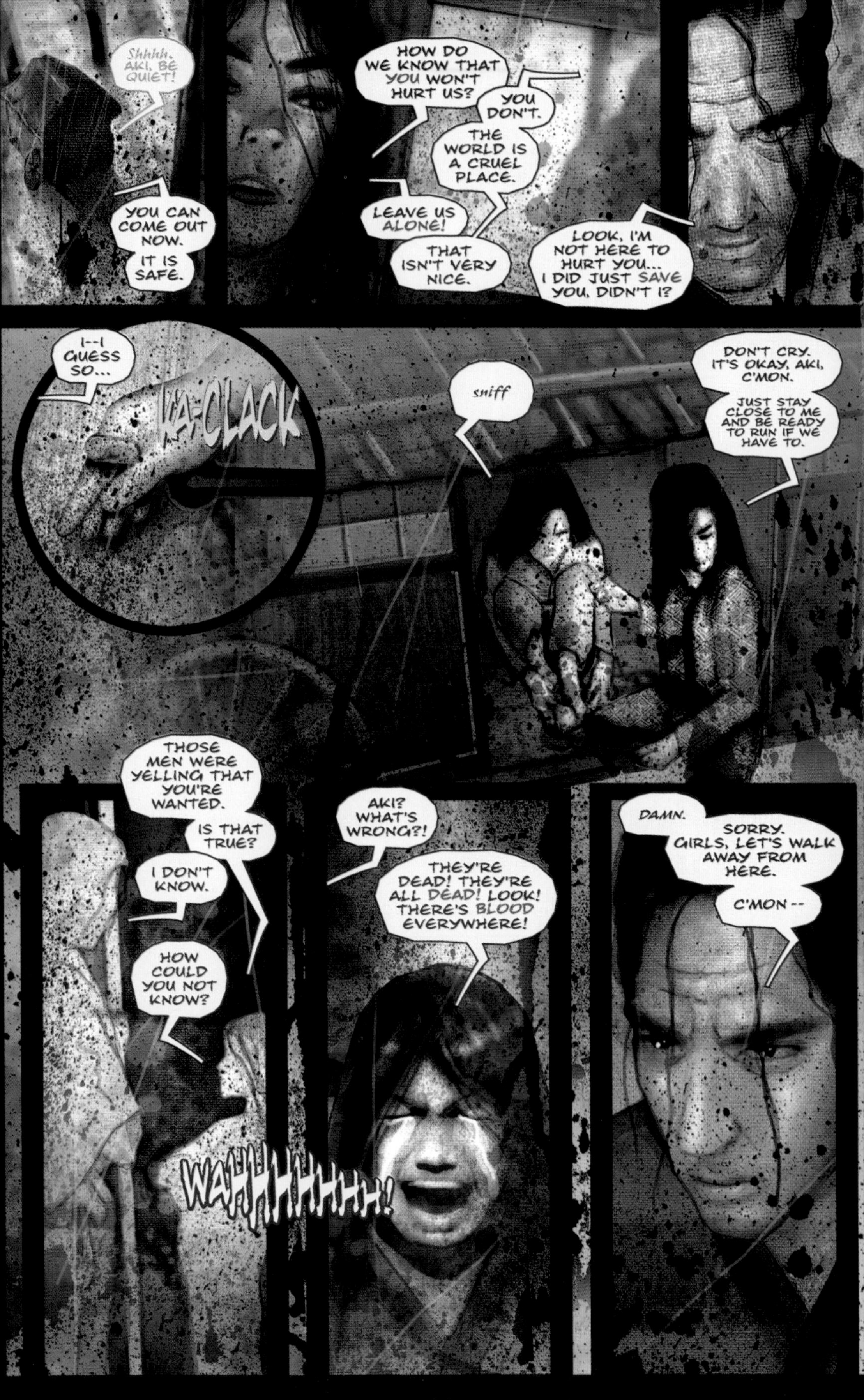

Shhhh. AKI, BE QUIET!
YOU CAN COME OUT NOW.
IT IS SAFE.
HOW DO WE KNOW THAT YOU WON'T HURT US?
YOU DON'T.
THE WORLD IS A CRUEL PLACE.
LEAVE US ALONE!
THAT ISN'T VERY NICE.
LOOK, I'M NOT HERE TO HURT YOU... I DID JUST SAVE YOU, DIDN'T I?
I--I GUESS SO...
KA-CLACK
sniff
DON'T CRY. IT'S OKAY, AKI, C'MON.
JUST STAY CLOSE TO ME AND BE READY TO RUN IF WE HAVE TO.
THOSE MEN WERE YELLING THAT YOU'RE WANTED.
IS THAT TRUE?
I DON'T KNOW.
HOW COULD YOU NOT KNOW?
WAHHHHHHH!
AKI? WHAT'S WRONG?!
THEY'RE DEAD! THEY'RE ALL DEAD! LOOK! THERE'S BLOOD EVERYWHERE!
DAMN.
SORRY. GIRLS, LET'S WALK AWAY FROM HERE.
C'MON --

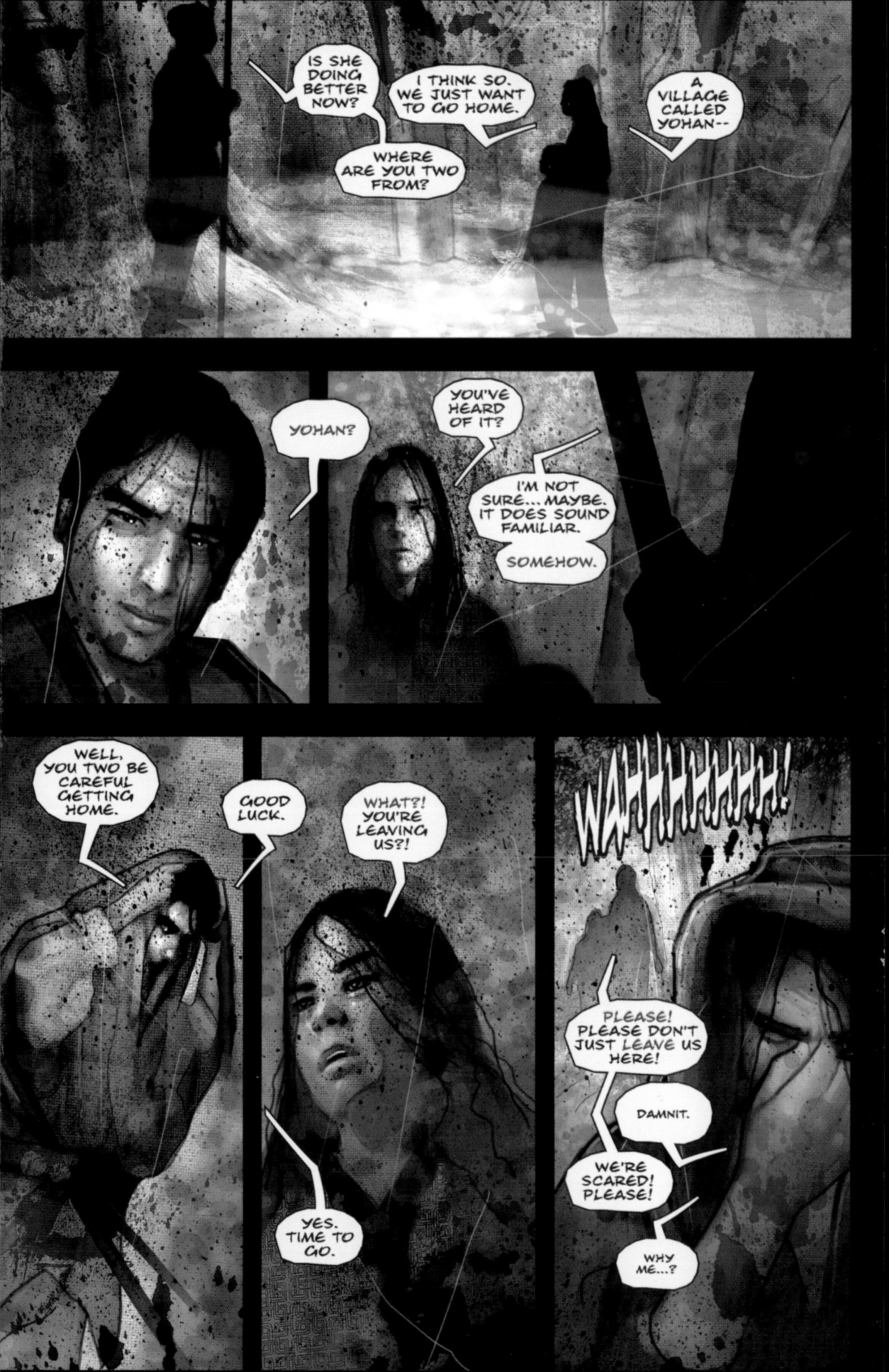

IS SHE DOING BETTER NOW?
I THINK SO. WE JUST WANT TO GO HOME.
WHERE ARE YOU TWO FROM?
A VILLAGE CALLED YOHAN--
YOHAN?
YOU'VE HEARD OF IT?
I'M NOT SURE... MAYBE. IT DOES SOUND FAMILIAR.
SOMEHOW.
WELL, YOU TWO BE CAREFUL GETTING HOME.
GOOD LUCK.
WHAT?! YOU'RE LEAVING US?!
YES. TIME TO GO.
WAHHHHHHH!
PLEASE! PLEASE DON'T JUST LEAVE US HERE!
DAMNIT.
WE'RE SCARED! PLEASE!
WHY ME...?

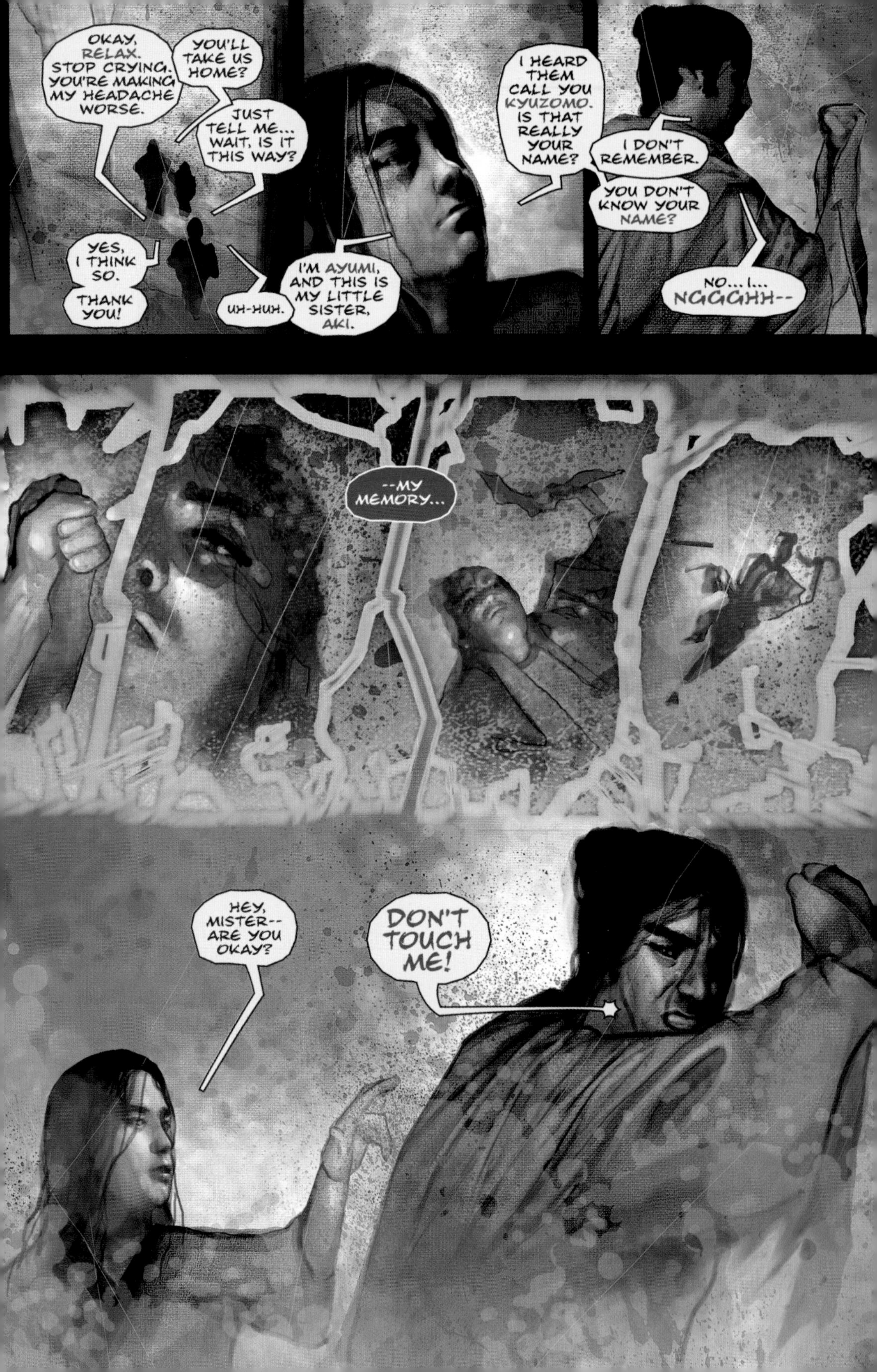
OKAY, RELAX. STOP CRYING. YOU'RE MAKING MY HEADACHE WORSE.
YOU'LL TAKE US HOME?
JUST TELL ME... WAIT, IS IT THIS WAY?
YES, I THINK SO.
THANK YOU!
UH-HUH.
I'M AYUMI, AND THIS IS MY LITTLE SISTER, AKI.
I HEARD THEM CALL YOU KYUZOMO. IS THAT REALLY YOUR NAME?
I DON'T REMEMBER.
YOU DON'T KNOW YOUR NAME?
NO... I... NGGGHH--
--MY MEMORY...
HEY, MISTER-- ARE YOU OKAY?
DON'T TOUCH ME!

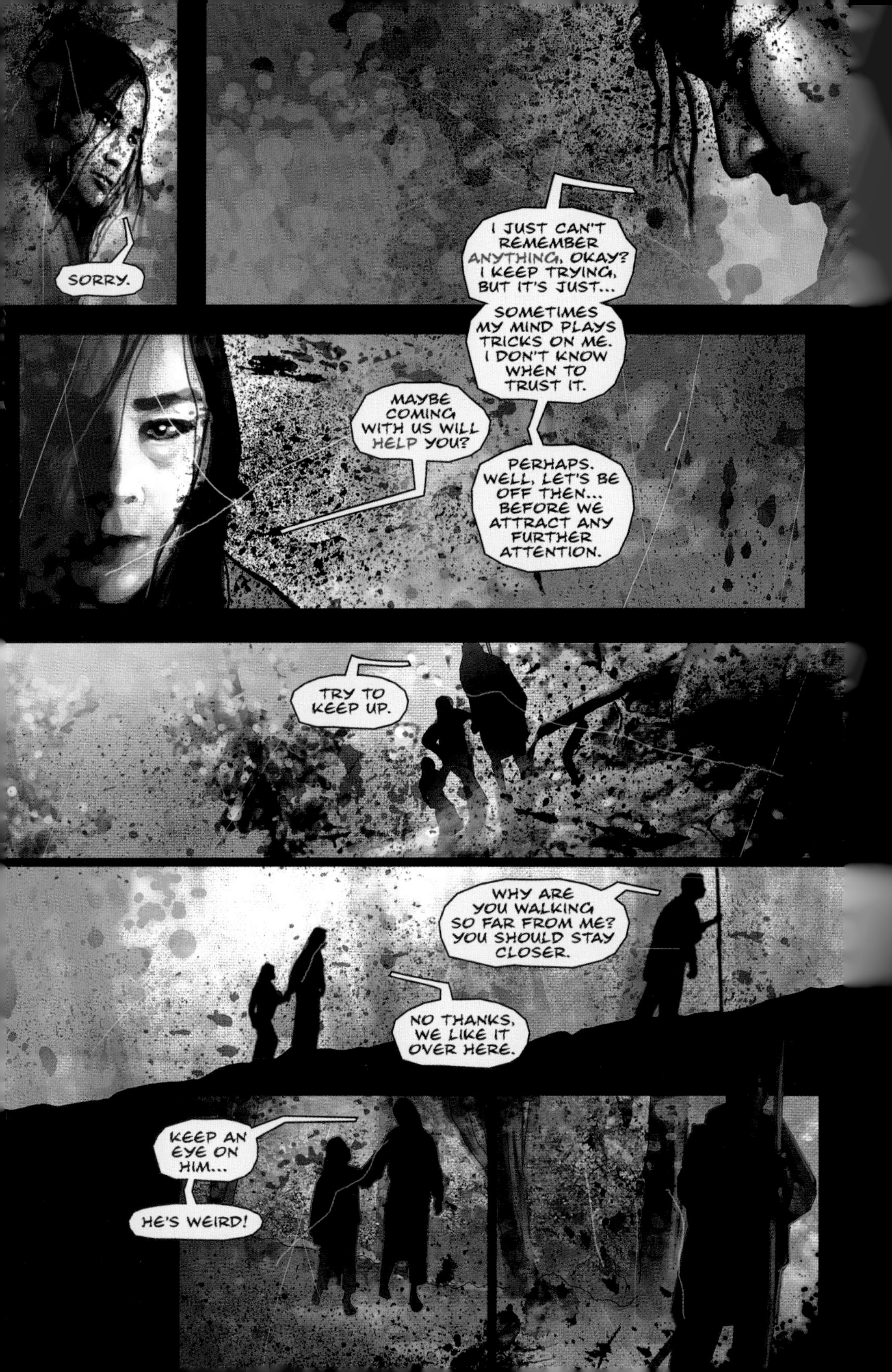
SORRY.
I JUST CAN'T REMEMBER ANYTHING, OKAY? I KEEP TRYING, BUT IT'S JUST...
SOMETIMES MY MIND PLAYS TRICKS ON ME. I DON'T KNOW WHEN TO TRUST IT.
MAYBE COMING WITH US WILL HELP YOU?
PERHAPS. WELL, LET'S BE OFF THEN... BEFORE WE ATTRACT ANY FURTHER ATTENTION.
TRY TO KEEP UP.
WHY ARE YOU WALKING SO FAR FROM ME? YOU SHOULD STAY CLOSER.
NO THANKS, WE LIKE IT OVER HERE.
KEEP AN EYE ON HIM...
HE'S WEIRD!

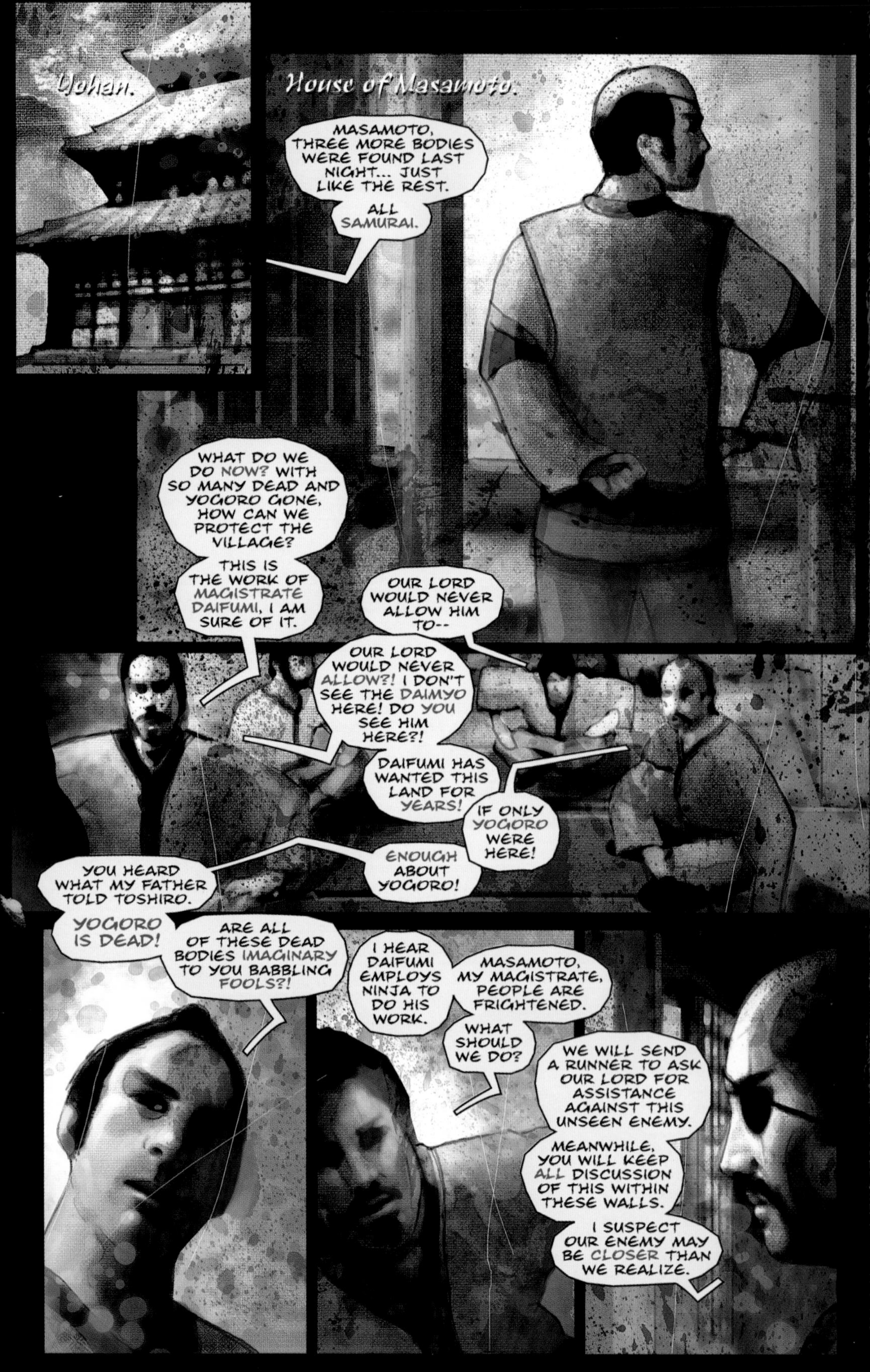
Uohan.
House of Masamoto.
MASAMOTO, THREE MORE BODIES WERE FOUND LAST NIGHT... JUST LIKE THE REST.
ALL SAMURAI.
WHAT DO WE DO NOW? WITH SO MANY DEAD AND YOGORO GONE, HOW CAN WE PROTECT THE VILLAGE?
THIS IS THE WORK OF MAGISTRATE DAIFUMI, I AM SURE OF IT.
OUR LORD WOULD NEVER ALLOW HIM TO--
OUR LORD WOULD NEVER ALLOW?! I DON'T SEE THE DAIMYO HERE! DO YOU SEE HIM HERE?!
DAIFUMI HAS WANTED THIS LAND FOR YEARS!
IF ONLY YOGORO WERE HERE!
ENOUGH ABOUT YOGORO!
YOU HEARD WHAT MY FATHER TOLD TOSHIRO.
YOGORO IS DEAD!
ARE ALL OF THESE DEAD BODIES IMAGINARY TO YOU BABBLING FOOLS?!
I HEAR DAIFUMI EMPLOYS NINJA TO DO HIS WORK.
MASAMOTO, MY MAGISTRATE, PEOPLE ARE FRIGHTENED.
WHAT SHOULD WE DO?
WE WILL SEND A RUNNER TO ASK OUR LORD FOR ASSISTANCE AGAINST THIS UNSEEN ENEMY.
MEANWHILE, YOU WILL KEEP ALL DISCUSSION OF THIS WITHIN THESE WALLS.
I SUSPECT OUR ENEMY MAY BE CLOSER THAN WE REALIZE.

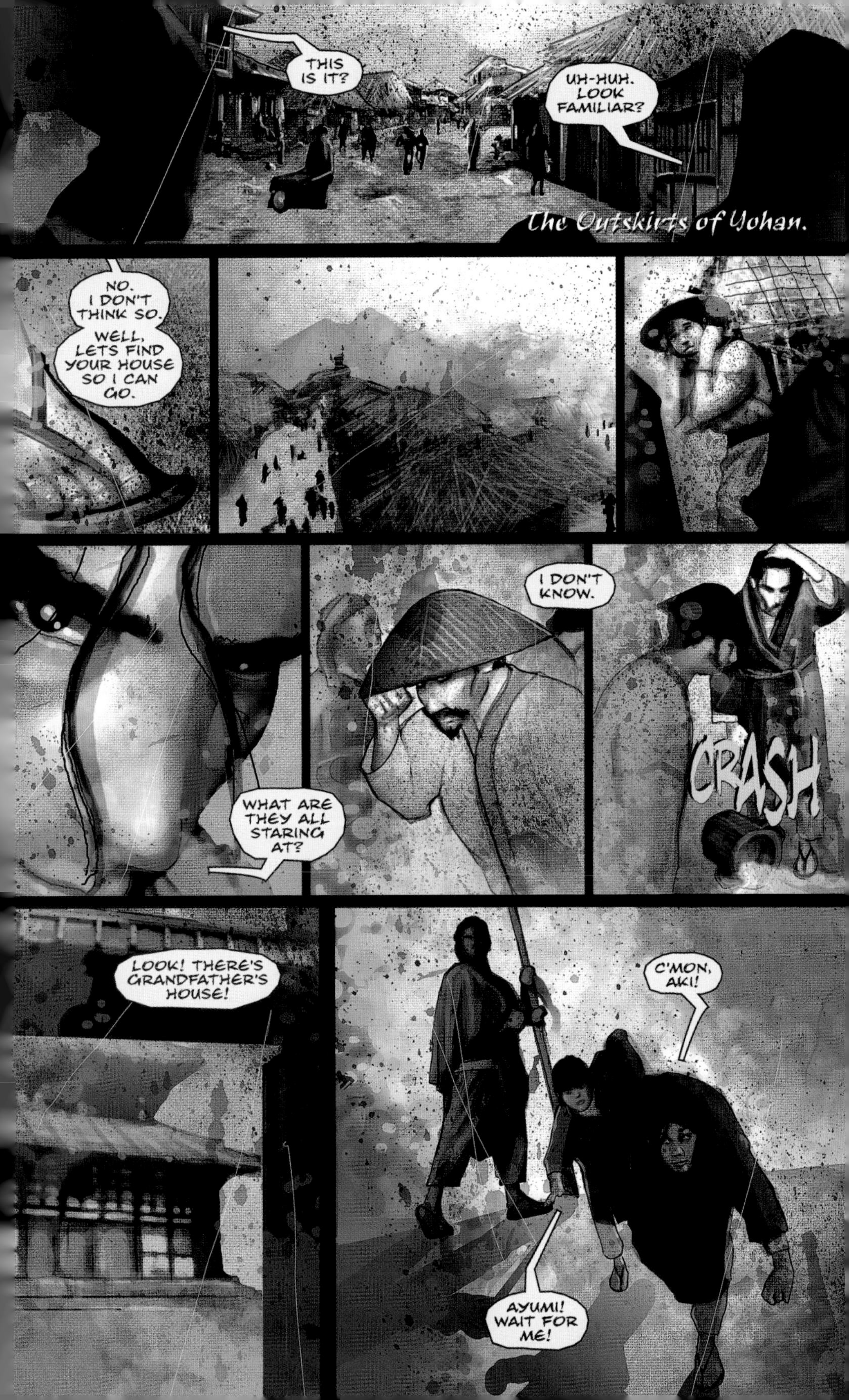
THIS IS IT?
UH-HUH. LOOK FAMILIAR?
The Outskirts of Yohan.
NO. I DON'T THINK SO.
WELL, LETS FIND YOUR HOUSE SO I CAN GO.
WHAT ARE THEY ALL STARING AT?
I DON'T KNOW.
CRASH
LOOK! THERE'S GRANDFATHER'S HOUSE!
C'MON, AKI!
AYUMI! WAIT FOR ME!

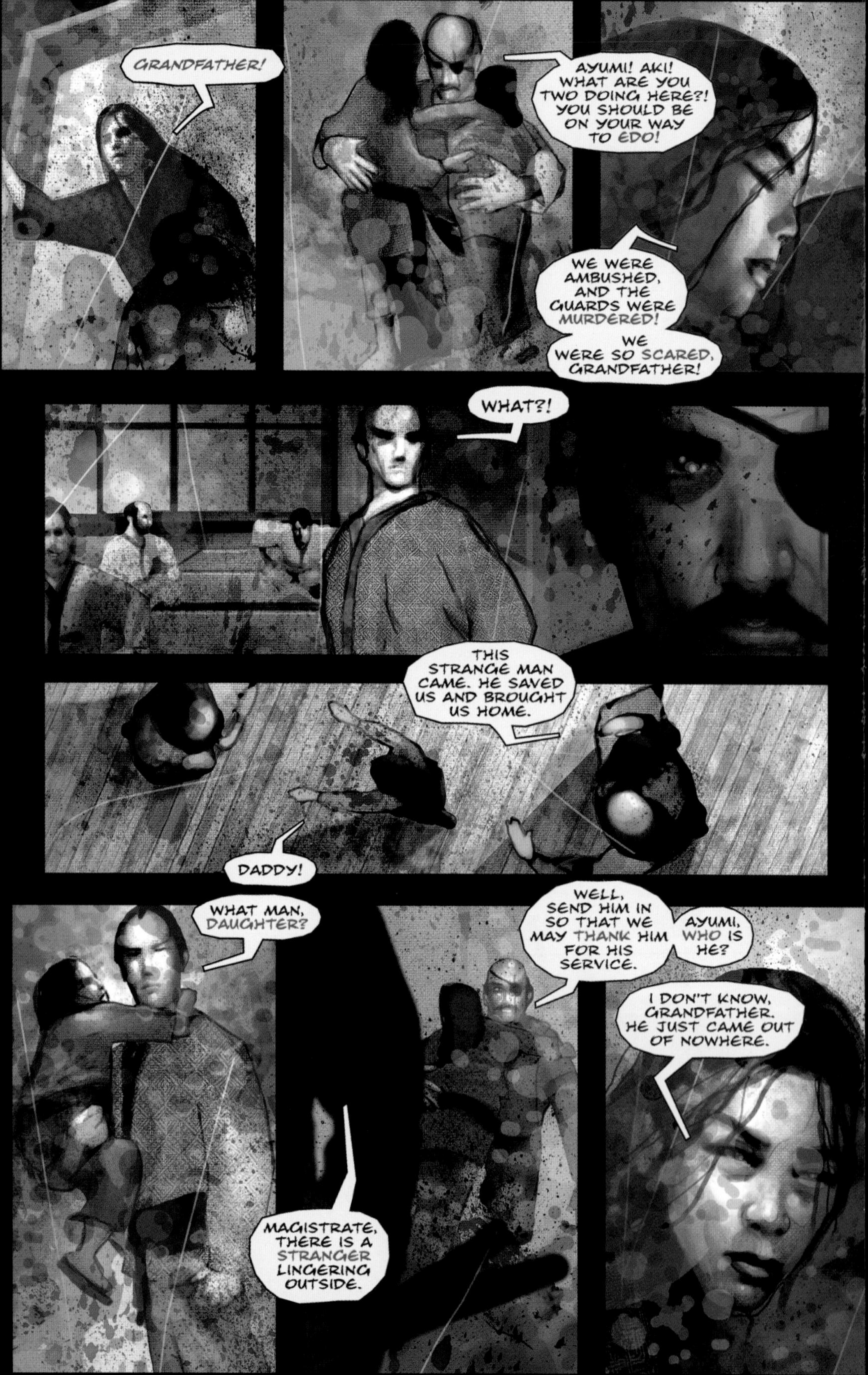
GRANDFATHER!
AYUMI! AKI! WHAT ARE YOU TWO DOING HERE?! YOU SHOULD BE ON YOUR WAY TO EDO!
WE WERE AMBUSHED, AND THE GUARDS WERE MURDERED!
WE WERE SO SCARED, GRANDFATHER!
WHAT?!
THIS STRANGE MAN CAME. HE SAVED US AND BROUGHT US HOME.
DADDY!
WHAT MAN, DAUGHTER?
WELL, SEND HIM IN SO THAT WE MAY THANK HIM FOR HIS SERVICE.
AYUMI, WHO IS HE?
I DON'T KNOW, GRANDFATHER. HE JUST CAME OUT OF NOWHERE.
MAGISTRATE, THERE IS A STRANGER LINGERING OUTSIDE.

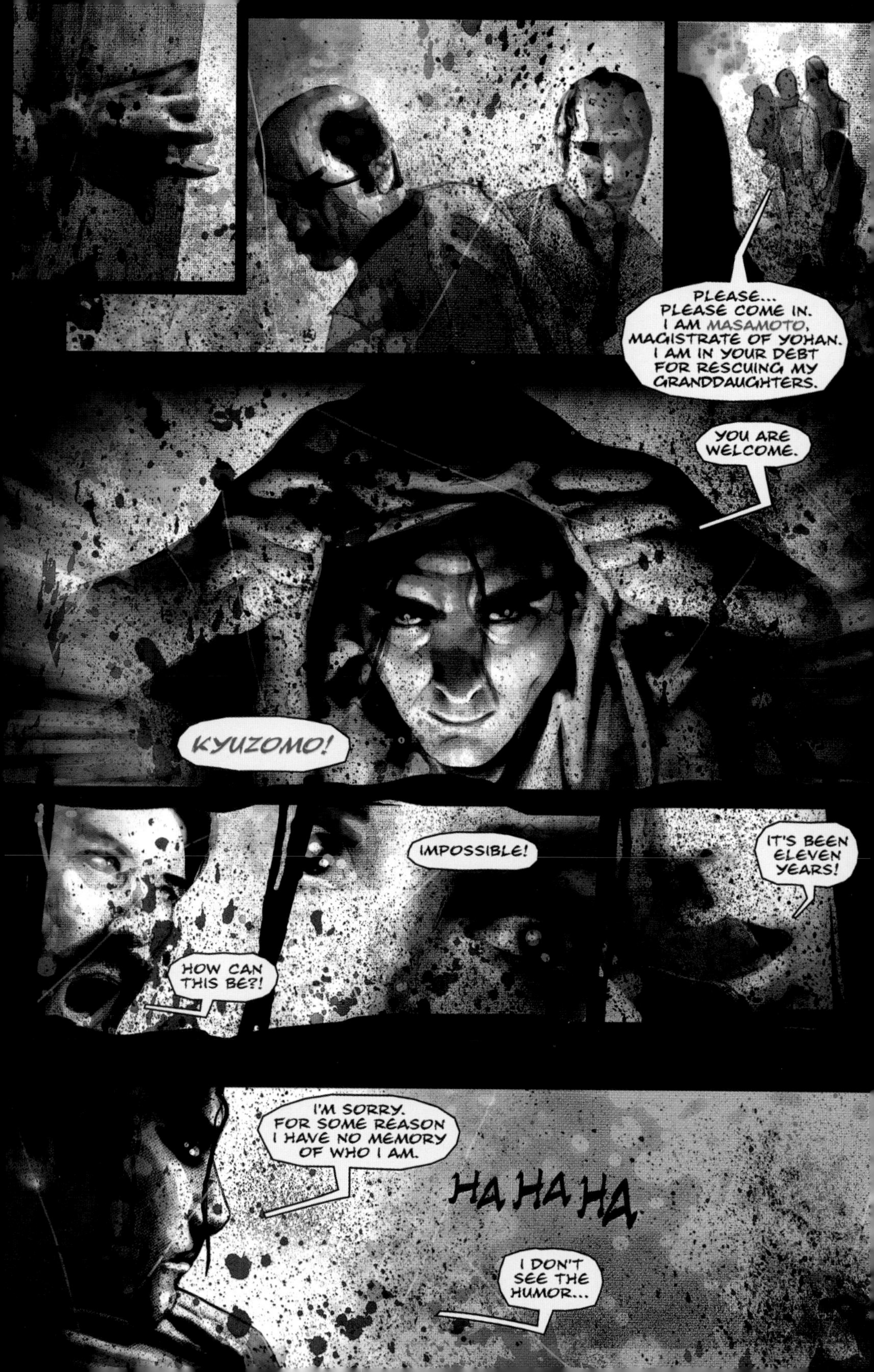
PLEASE... PLEASE COME IN. I AM MASAMOTO, MAGISTRATE OF YOHAN. I AM IN YOUR DEBT FOR RESCUING MY GRANDDAUGHTERS.
YOU ARE WELCOME.
KYUZOMO!
IMPOSSIBLE!
IT'S BEEN ELEVEN YEARS!
HOW CAN THIS BE?!
I'M SORRY. FOR SOME REASON I HAVE NO MEMORY OF WHO I AM.
HA HA HA
I DON'T SEE THE HUMOR...

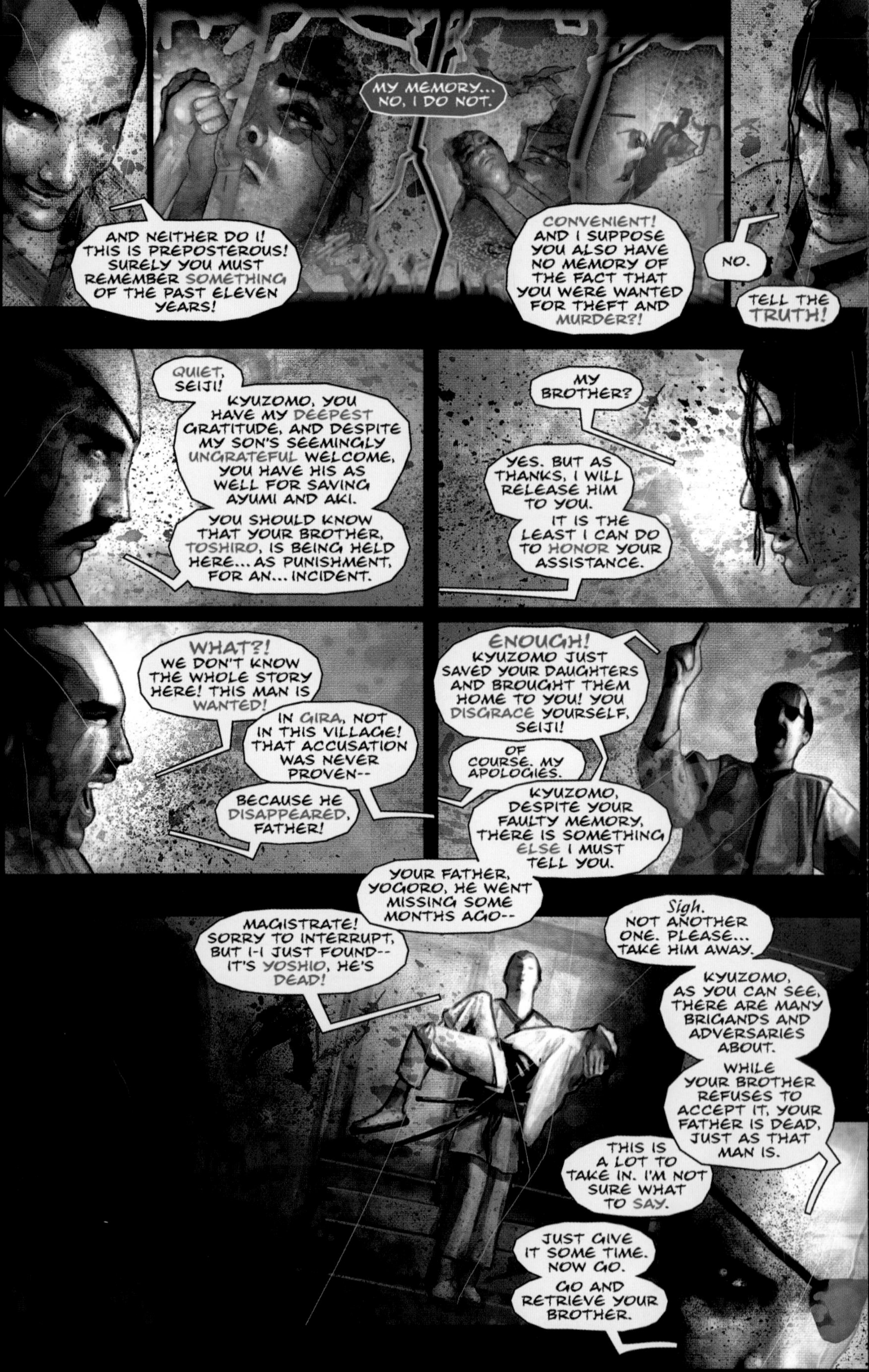
MY MEMORY... NO, I DO NOT.
AND NEITHER DO I! THIS IS PREPOSTEROUS! SURELY YOU MUST REMEMBER SOMETHING OF THE PAST ELEVEN YEARS!
CONVENIENT! AND I SUPPOSE YOU ALSO HAVE NO MEMORY OF THE FACT THAT YOU WERE WANTED FOR THEFT AND MURDER?!
NO.
TELL THE TRUTH!
QUIET, SEIJI!
KYUZOMO, YOU HAVE MY DEEPEST GRATITUDE, AND DESPITE MY SON'S SEEMINGLY UNGRATEFUL WELCOME, YOU HAVE HIS AS WELL FOR SAVING AYUMI AND AKI.
YOU SHOULD KNOW THAT YOUR BROTHER, TOSHIRO, IS BEING HELD HERE... AS PUNISHMENT, FOR AN... INCIDENT.
MY BROTHER?
YES. BUT AS THANKS, I WILL RELEASE HIM TO YOU.
IT IS THE LEAST I CAN DO TO HONOR YOUR ASSISTANCE.
WHAT?! WE DON'T KNOW THE WHOLE STORY HERE! THIS MAN IS WANTED!
IN GIRA, NOT IN THIS VILLAGE! THAT ACCUSATION WAS NEVER PROVEN--
BECAUSE HE DISAPPEARED, FATHER!
ENOUGH! KYUZOMO JUST SAVED YOUR DAUGHTERS AND BROUGHT THEM HOME TO YOU! YOU DISGRACE YOURSELF, SEIJI!
OF COURSE. MY APOLOGIES.
KYUZOMO, DESPITE YOUR FAULTY MEMORY, THERE IS SOMETHING ELSE I MUST TELL YOU.
YOUR FATHER, YOGORO, HE WENT MISSING SOME MONTHS AGO--
MAGISTRATE! SORRY TO INTERRUPT, BUT I-I JUST FOUND-- IT'S YOSHIO, HE'S DEAD!
Sigh. NOT ANOTHER ONE. PLEASE... TAKE HIM AWAY.
KYUZOMO, AS YOU CAN SEE, THERE ARE MANY BRIGANDS AND ADVERSARIES ABOUT.
WHILE YOUR BROTHER REFUSES TO ACCEPT IT, YOUR FATHER IS DEAD, JUST AS THAT MAN IS.
THIS IS A LOT TO TAKE IN. I'M NOT SURE WHAT TO SAY.
JUST GIVE IT SOME TIME. NOW GO.
GO AND RETRIEVE YOUR BROTHER.

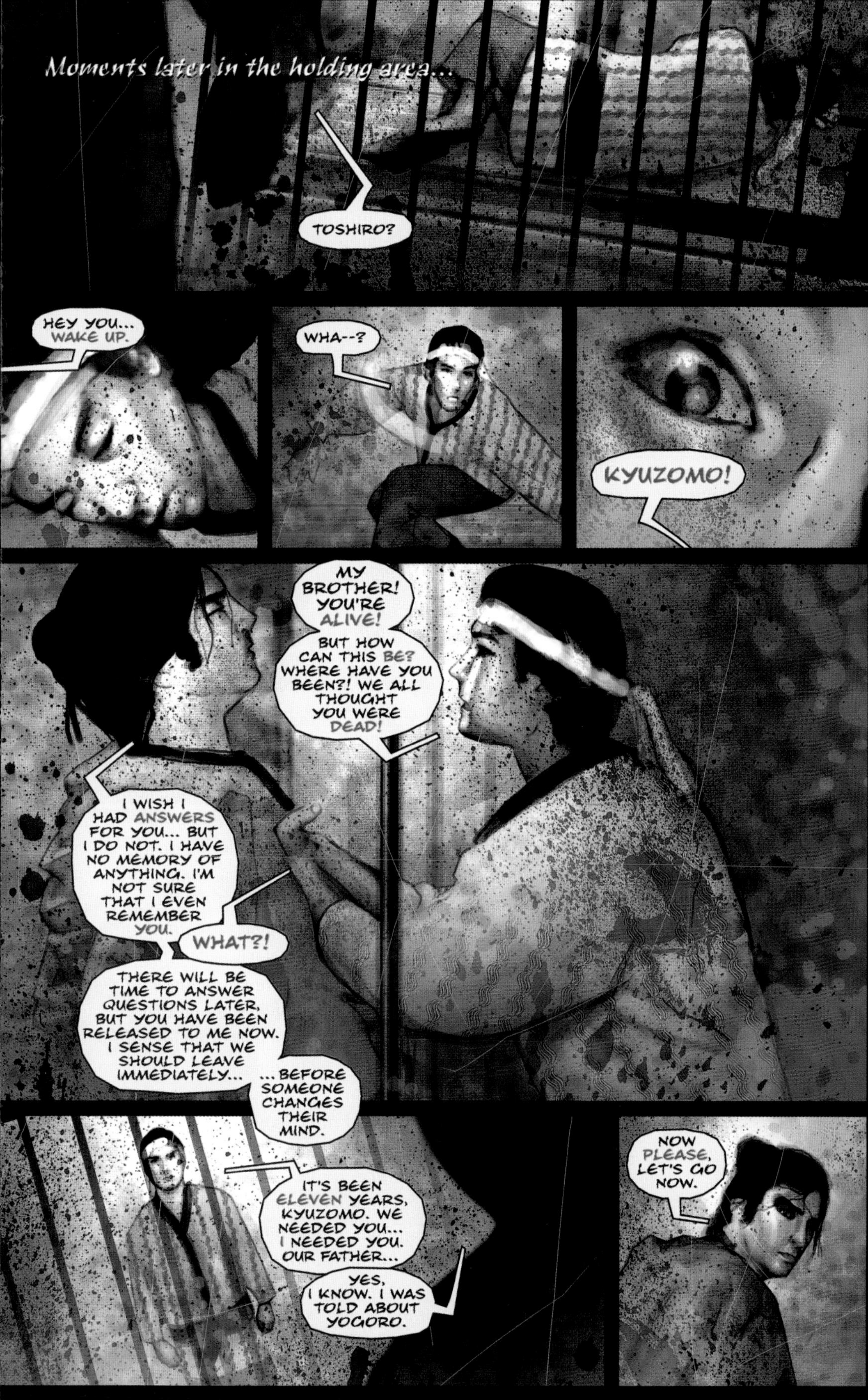
Moments later in the holding area...
TOSHIRO?
HEY YOU... WAKE UP.
WHA--?
KYUZOMO!
MY BROTHER! YOU'RE ALIVE!
BUT HOW CAN THIS BE? WHERE HAVE YOU BEEN?! WE ALL THOUGHT YOU WERE DEAD!
I WISH I HAD ANSWERS FOR YOU... BUT I DO NOT. I HAVE NO MEMORY OF ANYTHING. I'M NOT SURE THAT I EVEN REMEMBER YOU.
WHAT?!
THERE WILL BE TIME TO ANSWER QUESTIONS LATER, BUT YOU HAVE BEEN RELEASED TO ME NOW. I SENSE THAT WE SHOULD LEAVE IMMEDIATELY...
...BEFORE SOMEONE CHANGES THEIR MIND.
IT'S BEEN ELEVEN YEARS, KYUZOMO. WE NEEDED YOU... I NEEDED YOU. OUR FATHER...
YES, I KNOW. I WAS TOLD ABOUT YOGORO.
NOW PLEASE, LET'S GO NOW.

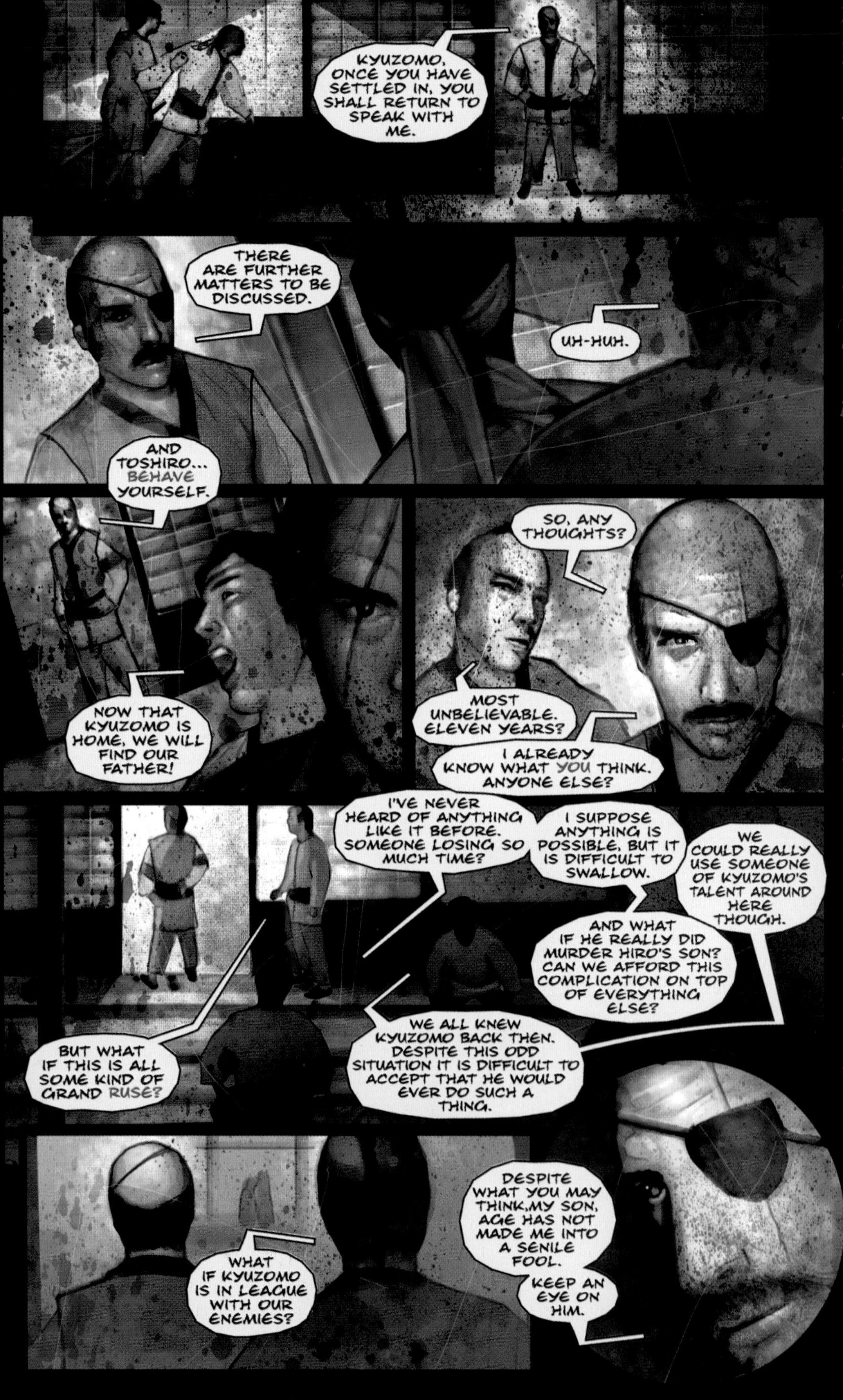
KYUZOMO, ONCE YOU HAVE SETTLED IN, YOU SHALL RETURN TO SPEAK WITH ME.
THERE ARE FURTHER MATTERS TO BE DISCUSSED.
UH-HUH.
AND TOSHIRO... BEHAVE YOURSELF.
NOW THAT KYUZOMO IS HOME, WE WILL FIND OUR FATHER!
SO, ANY THOUGHTS?
MOST UNBELIEVABLE. ELEVEN YEARS?
I ALREADY KNOW WHAT YOU THINK. ANYONE ELSE?
I'VE NEVER HEARD OF ANYTHING LIKE IT BEFORE. SOMEONE LOSING SO MUCH TIME?
I SUPPOSE ANYTHING IS POSSIBLE, BUT IT IS DIFFICULT TO SWALLOW.
WE COULD REALLY USE SOMEONE OF KYUZOMO'S TALENT AROUND HERE THOUGH.
AND WHAT IF HE REALLY DID MURDER HIRO'S SON? CAN WE AFFORD THIS COMPLICATION ON TOP OF EVERYTHING ELSE?
WE ALL KNEW KYUZOMO BACK THEN. DESPITE THIS ODD SITUATION IT IS DIFFICULT TO ACCEPT THAT HE WOULD EVER DO SUCH A THING.
BUT WHAT IF THIS IS ALL SOME KIND OF GRAND RUSE?
WHAT IF KYUZOMO IS IN LEAGUE WITH OUR ENEMIES?
DESPITE WHAT YOU MAY THINK,MY SON, AGE HAS NOT MADE ME INTO A SENILE FOOL.
KEEP AN EYE ON HIM.

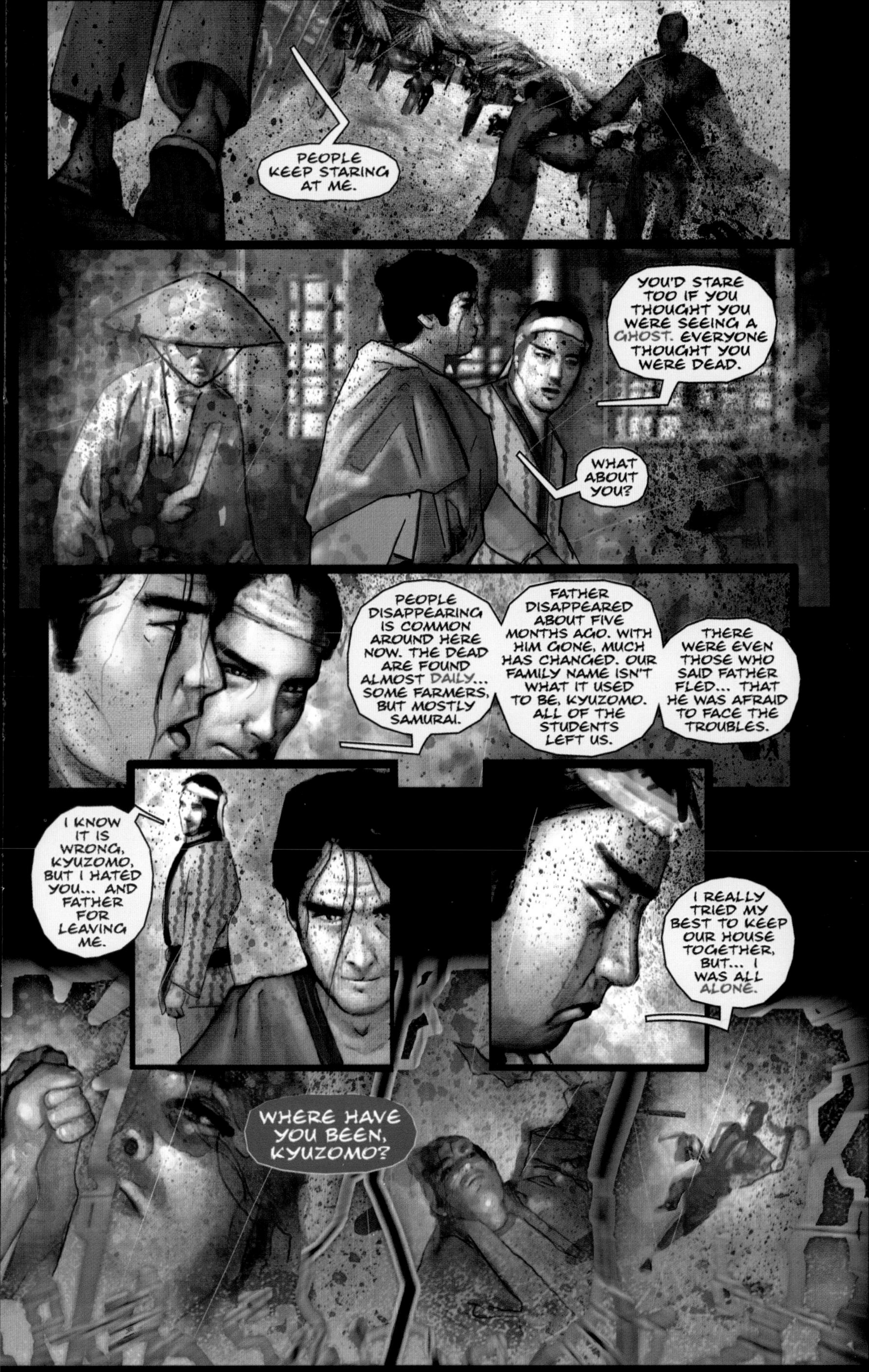
PEOPLE KEEP STARING AT ME.
YOU'D STARE TOO IF YOU THOUGHT YOU WERE SEEING A GHOST. EVERYONE THOUGHT YOU WERE DEAD.
WHAT ABOUT YOU?
PEOPLE DISAPPEARING IS COMMON AROUND HERE NOW. THE DEAD ARE FOUND ALMOST DAILY... SOME FARMERS, BUT MOSTLY SAMURAI.
FATHER DISAPPEARED ABOUT FIVE MONTHS AGO. WITH HIM GONE, MUCH HAS CHANGED. OUR FAMILY NAME ISN'T WHAT IT USED TO BE, KYUZOMO. ALL OF THE STUDENTS LEFT US.
THERE WERE EVEN THOSE WHO SAID FATHER FLED... THAT HE WAS AFRAID TO FACE THE TROUBLES.
I KNOW IT IS WRONG, KYUZOMO, BUT I HATED YOU... AND FATHER FOR LEAVING ME.
I REALLY TRIED MY BEST TO KEEP OUR HOUSE TOGETHER, BUT... I WAS ALL ALONE.
WHERE HAVE YOU BEEN, KYUZOMO?

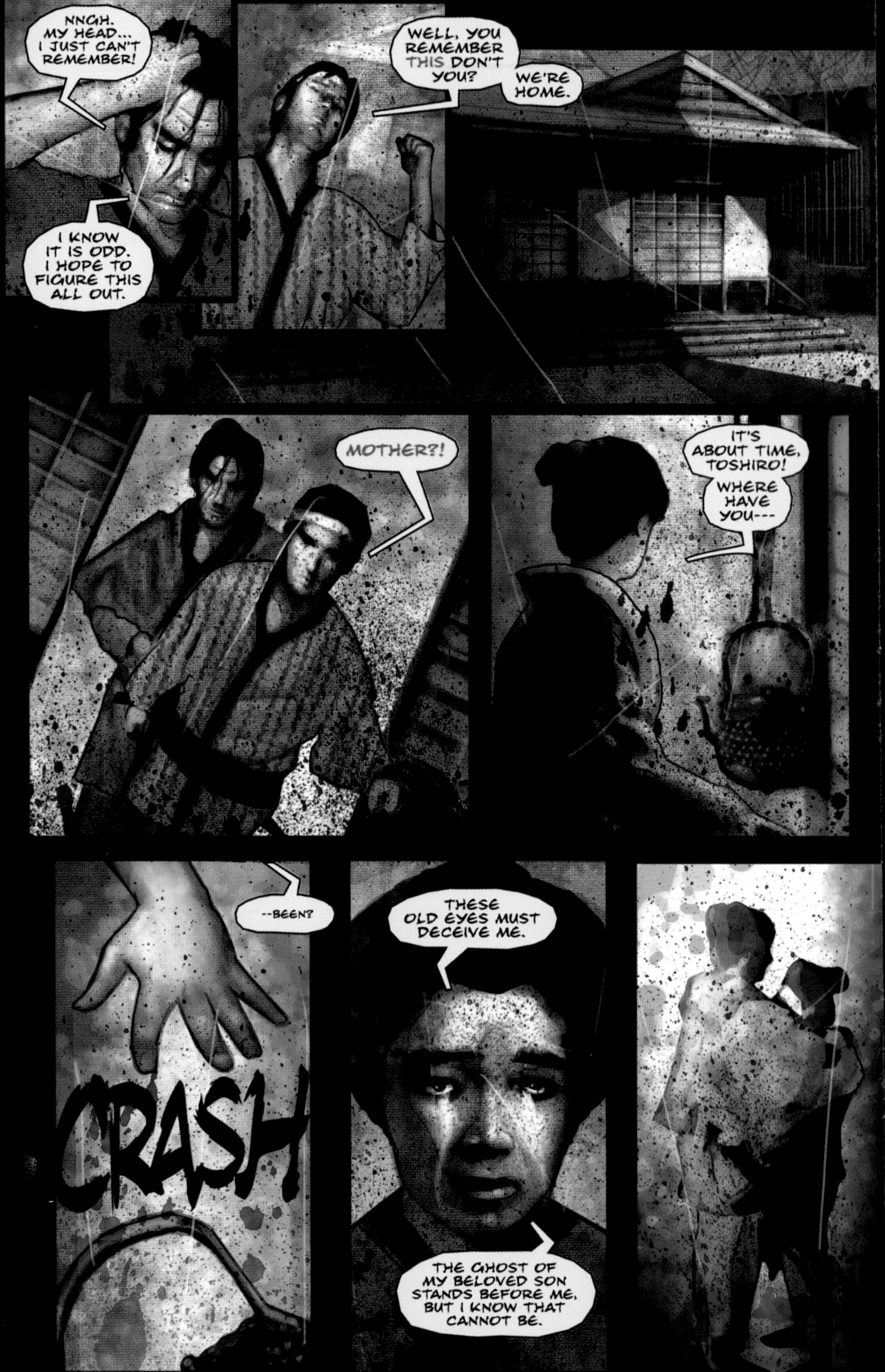
NNGH. MY HEAD... I JUST CAN'T REMEMBER!
I KNOW IT IS ODD. I HOPE TO FIGURE THIS ALL OUT.
WELL, YOU REMEMBER THIS DON'T YOU?
WE'RE HOME.
MOTHER?!
IT'S ABOUT TIME, TOSHIRO!
WHERE HAVE YOU---
--BEEN?
CRASH
THESE OLD EYES MUST DECEIVE ME.
THE GHOST OF MY BELOVED SON STANDS BEFORE ME, BUT I KNOW THAT CANNOT BE.

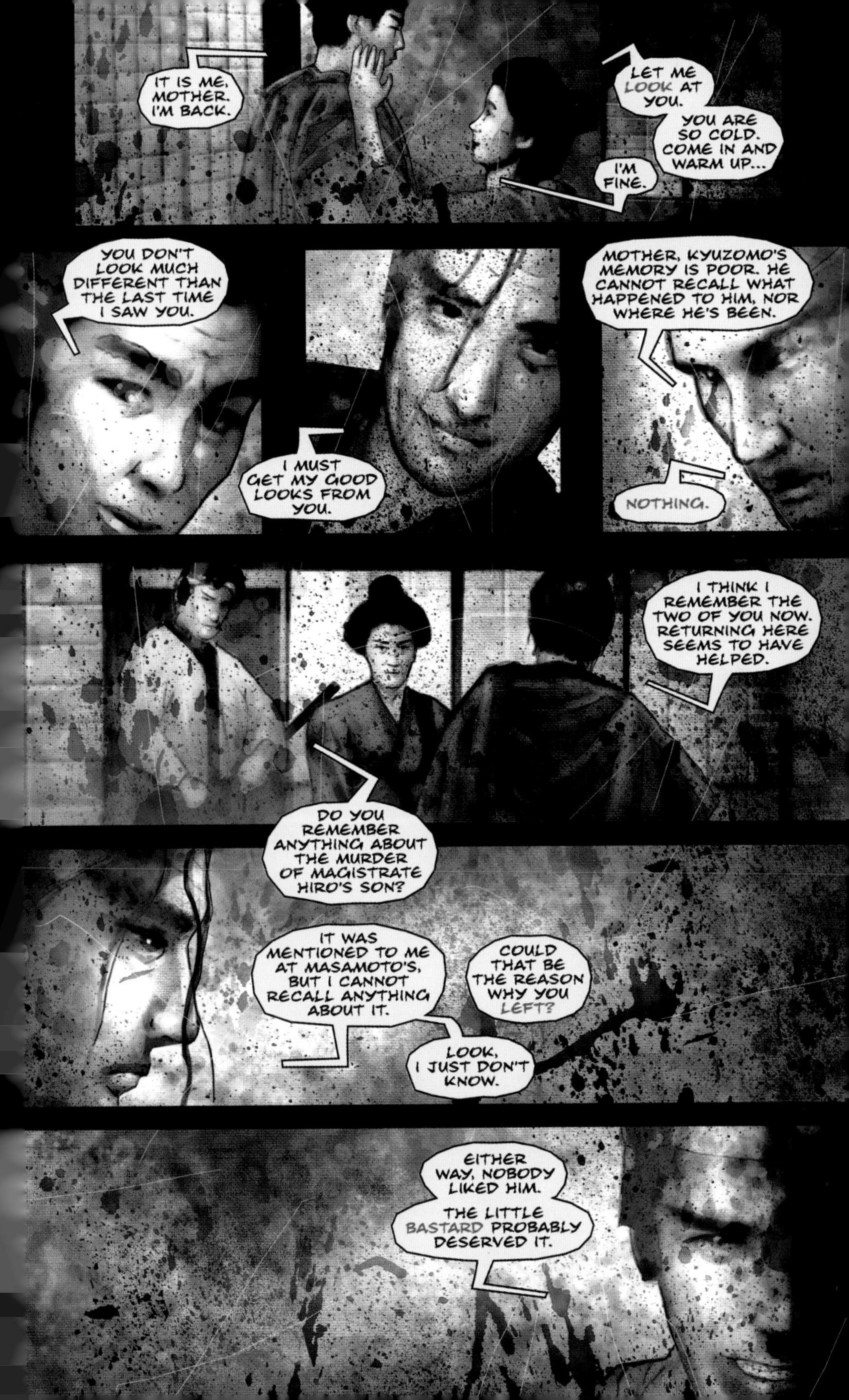
IT IS ME, MOTHER. I'M BACK.
LET ME LOOK AT YOU.
YOU ARE SO COLD. COME IN AND WARM UP...
I'M FINE.
YOU DON'T LOOK MUCH DIFFERENT THAN THE LAST TIME I SAW YOU.
I MUST GET MY GOOD LOOKS FROM YOU.
MOTHER, KYUZOMO'S MEMORY IS POOR. HE CANNOT RECALL WHAT HAPPENED TO HIM, NOR WHERE HE'S BEEN.
NOTHING.
I THINK I REMEMBER THE TWO OF YOU NOW. RETURNING HERE SEEMS TO HAVE HELPED.
DO YOU REMEMBER ANYTHING ABOUT THE MURDER OF MAGISTRATE HIRO'S SON?
IT WAS MENTIONED TO ME AT MASAMOTO'S, BUT I CANNOT RECALL ANYTHING ABOUT IT.
COULD THAT BE THE REASON WHY YOU LEFT?
LOOK, I JUST DON'T KNOW.
EITHER WAY, NOBODY LIKED HIM.
THE LITTLE BASTARD PROBABLY DESERVED IT.

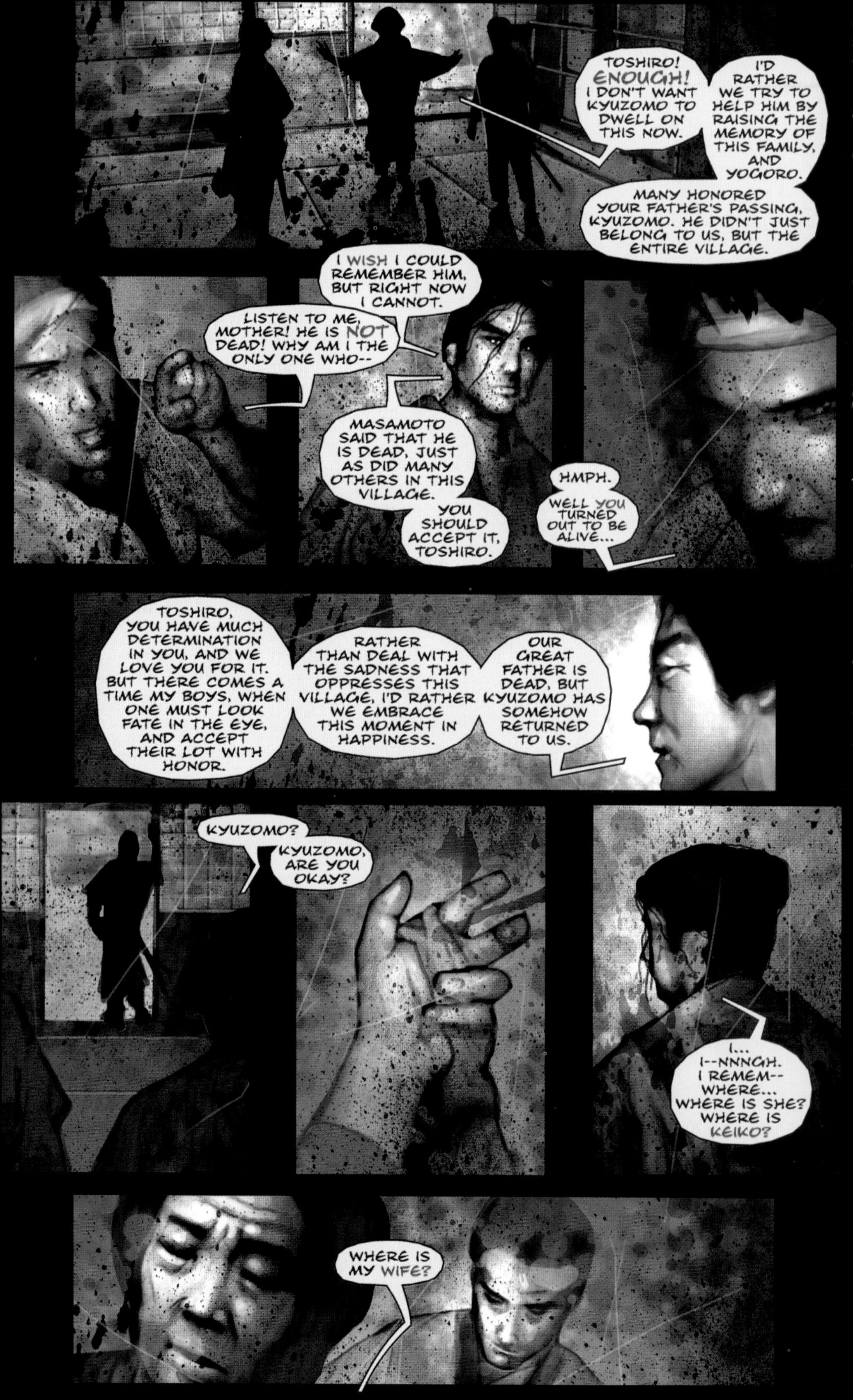

TOSHIRO! ENOUGH! I DON'T WANT KYUZOMO TO DWELL ON THIS NOW.
I'D RATHER WE TRY TO HELP HIM BY RAISING THE MEMORY OF THIS FAMILY, AND YOGORO.
MANY HONORED YOUR FATHER'S PASSING, KYUZOMO. HE DIDN'T JUST BELONG TO US, BUT THE ENTIRE VILLAGE.
I WISH I COULD REMEMBER HIM, BUT RIGHT NOW I CANNOT.
LISTEN TO ME, MOTHER! HE IS NOT DEAD! WHY AM I THE ONLY ONE WHO--
MASAMOTO SAID THAT HE IS DEAD, JUST AS DID MANY OTHERS IN THIS VILLAGE.
YOU SHOULD ACCEPT IT, TOSHIRO.
HMPH.
WELL YOU TURNED OUT TO BE ALIVE...
TOSHIRO, YOU HAVE MUCH DETERMINATION IN YOU, AND WE LOVE YOU FOR IT. BUT THERE COMES A TIME MY BOYS, WHEN ONE MUST LOOK FATE IN THE EYE, AND ACCEPT THEIR LOT WITH HONOR.
RATHER THAN DEAL WITH THE SADNESS THAT OPPRESSES THIS VILLAGE, I'D RATHER WE EMBRACE THIS MOMENT IN HAPPINESS.
OUR GREAT FATHER IS DEAD, BUT KYUZOMO HAS SOMEHOW RETURNED TO US.
KYUZOMO?
KYUZOMO, ARE YOU OKAY?
I... I--NNNGH. I REMEM-- WHERE... WHERE IS SHE? WHERE IS KEIKO?
WHERE IS MY WIFE?

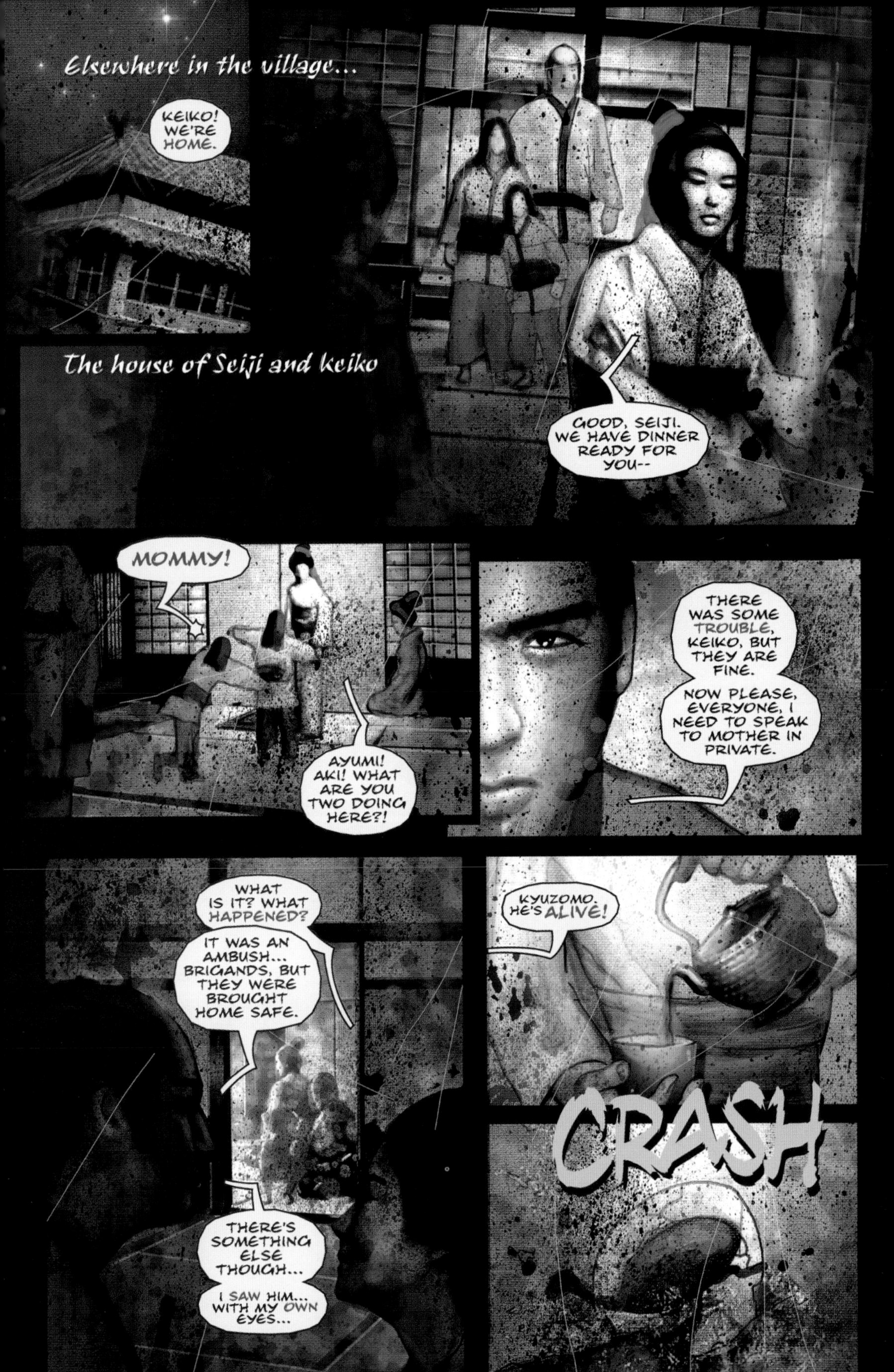
Elsewhere in the village...
KEIKO! WE'RE HOME.
The house of Seiji and keiko
GOOD, SEIJI. WE HAVE DINNER READY FOR YOU--
MOMMY!
AYUMI! AKI! WHAT ARE YOU TWO DOING HERE?!
THERE WAS SOME TROUBLE, KEIKO, BUT THEY ARE FINE.
NOW PLEASE, EVERYONE, I NEED TO SPEAK TO MOTHER IN PRIVATE.
WHAT IS IT? WHAT HAPPENED?
IT WAS AN AMBUSH... BRIGANDS, BUT THEY WERE BROUGHT HOME SAFE.
THERE'S SOMETHING ELSE THOUGH...
I SAW HIM... WITH MY OWN EYES...
KYUZOMO. HE'S ALIVE!
CRASH

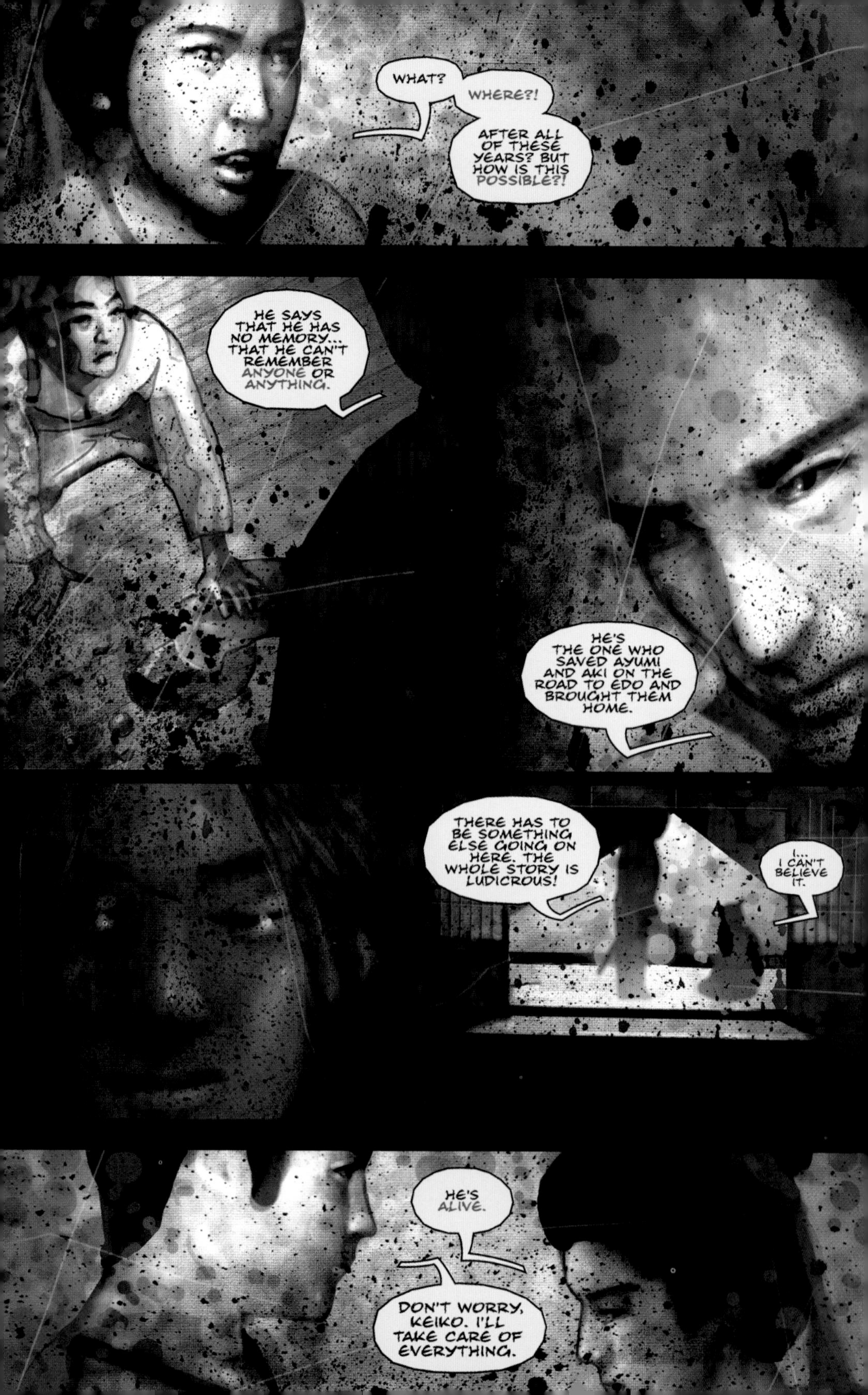
WHAT?
WHERE?!
AFTER ALL OF THESE YEARS? BUT HOW IS THIS POSSIBLE?!
HE SAYS THAT HE HAS NO MEMORY... THAT HE CAN'T REMEMBER ANYONE OR ANYTHING.
HE'S THE ONE WHO SAVED AYUMI AND AKI ON THE ROAD TO EDO AND BROUGHT THEM HOME.
THERE HAS TO BE SOMETHING ELSE GOING ON HERE. THE WHOLE STORY IS LUDICROUS!
I... I CAN'T BELIEVE IT.
HE'S ALIVE.
DON'T WORRY, KEIKO. I'LL TAKE CARE OF EVERYTHING.

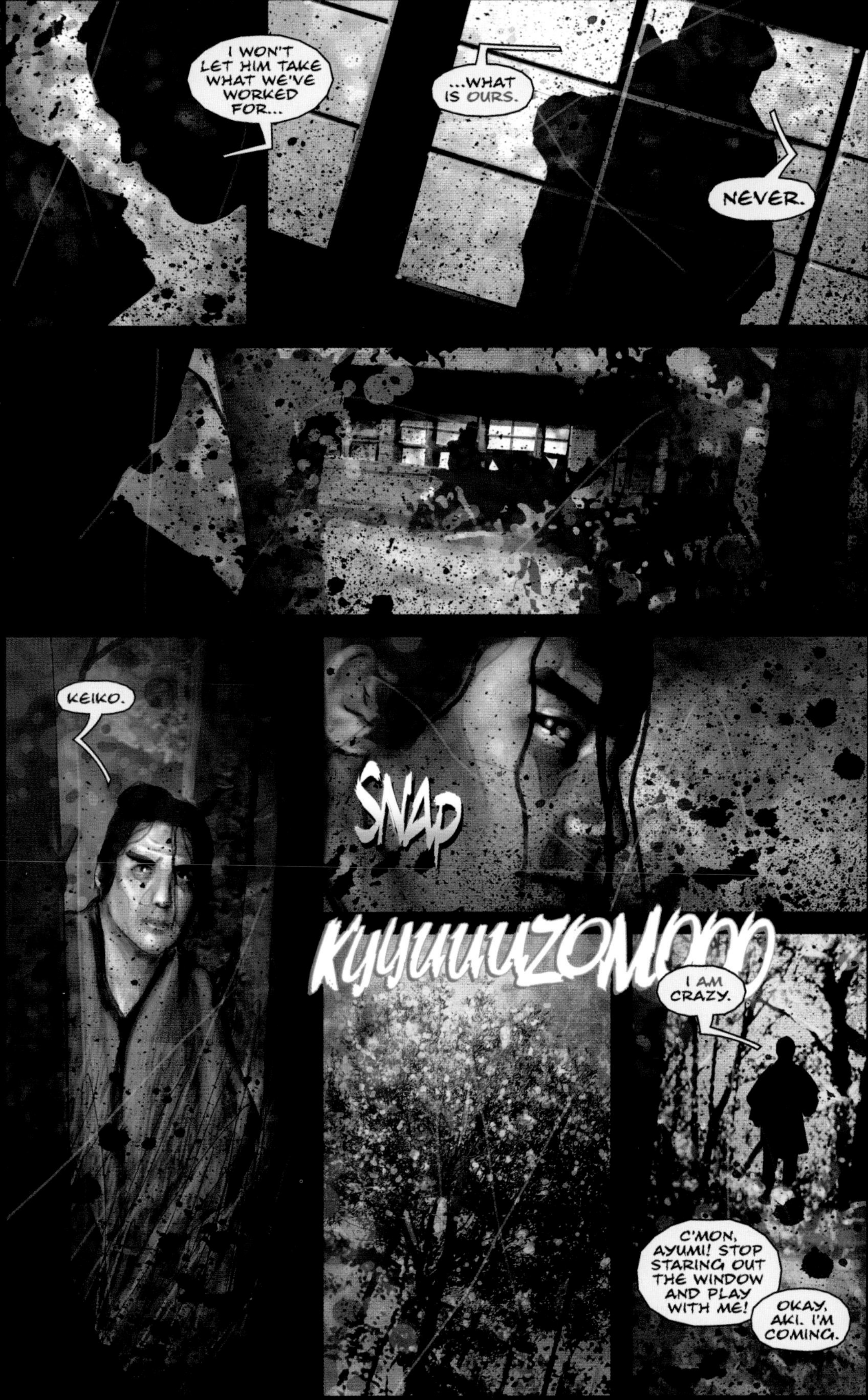
I WON'T LET HIM TAKE WHAT WE'VE WORKED FOR...
...WHAT IS OURS.
NEVER.
KEIKO.
SNAP
KYYUUUZOMOOO
I AM CRAZY.
C'MON, AYUMI! STOP STARING OUT THE WINDOW AND PLAY WITH ME!
OKAY, AKI. I'M COMING.

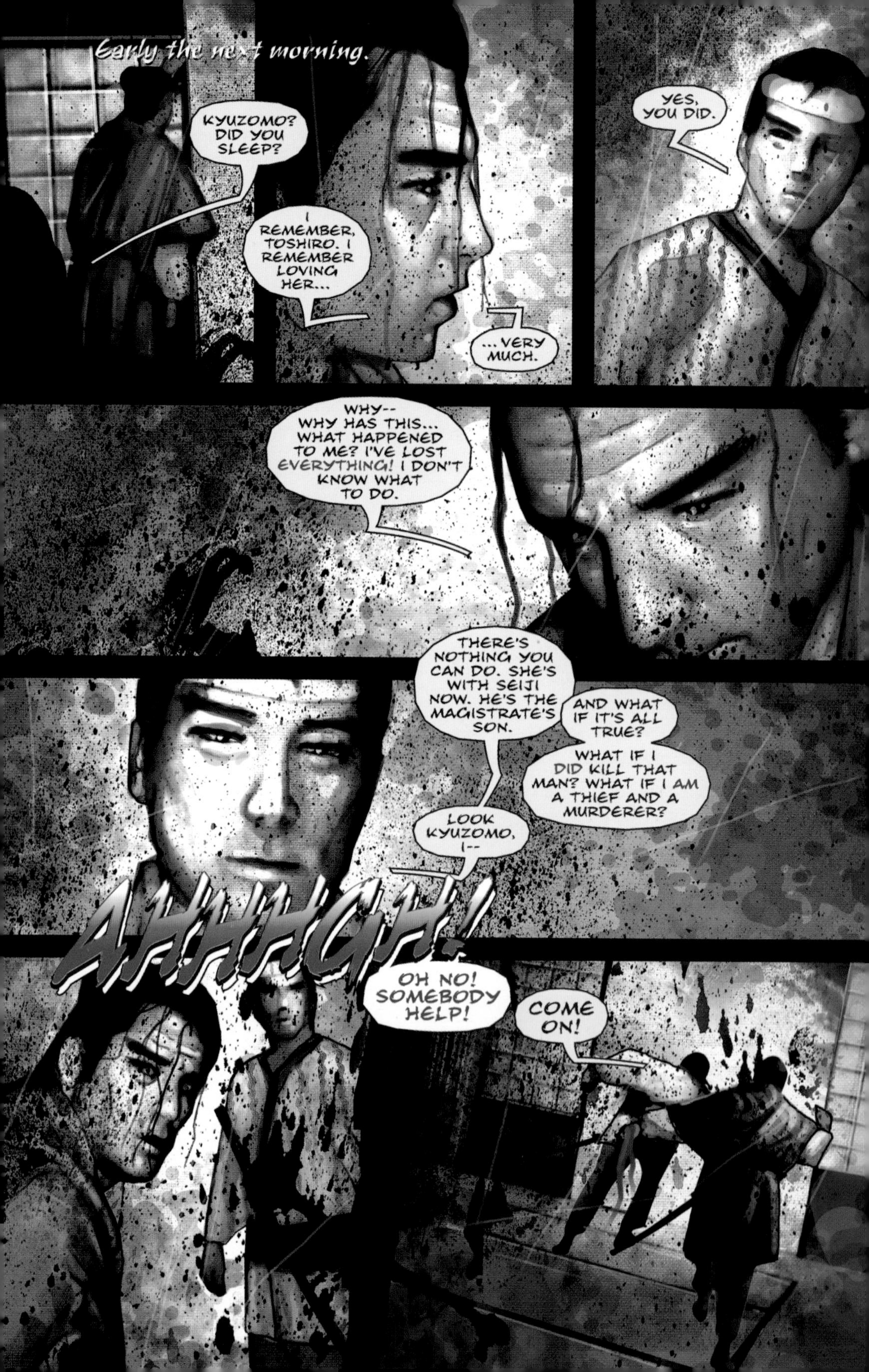
Early the next morning.
KYUZOMO? DID YOU SLEEP?
I REMEMBER, TOSHIRO. I REMEMBER LOVING HER...
...VERY MUCH.
YES, YOU DID.
WHY-- WHY HAS THIS... WHAT HAPPENED TO ME? I'VE LOST EVERYTHING! I DON'T KNOW WHAT TO DO.
THERE'S NOTHING YOU CAN DO. SHE'S WITH SEIJI NOW. HE'S THE MAGISTRATE'S SON.
AND WHAT IF IT'S ALL TRUE?
WHAT IF I DID KILL THAT MAN? WHAT IF I AM A THIEF AND A MURDERER?
LOOK KYUZOMO, I--
AHHHGH!
OH NO! SOMEBODY HELP!
COME ON!

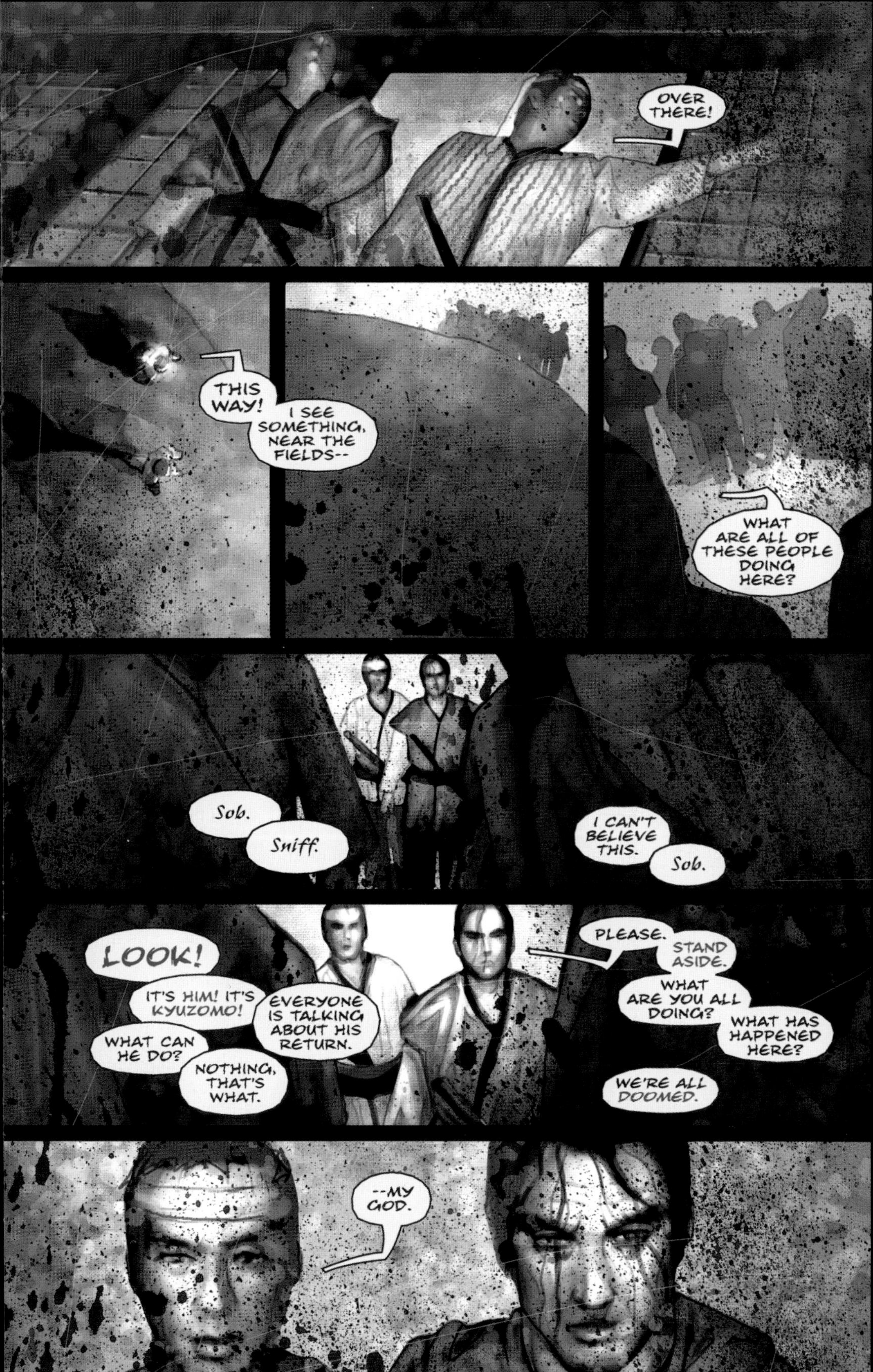
OVER THERE!
THIS WAY!
I SEE SOMETHING, NEAR THE FIELDS--
WHAT ARE ALL OF THESE PEOPLE DOING HERE?
Sob.
Sniff.
I CAN'T BELIEVE THIS.
Sob.
LOOK!
IT'S HIM! IT'S KYUZOMO!
EVERYONE IS TALKING ABOUT HIS RETURN.
WHAT CAN HE DO?
NOTHING, THAT'S WHAT.
PLEASE.
STAND ASIDE.
WHAT ARE YOU ALL DOING?
WHAT HAS HAPPENED HERE?
WE'RE ALL DOOMED.
--MY GOD.

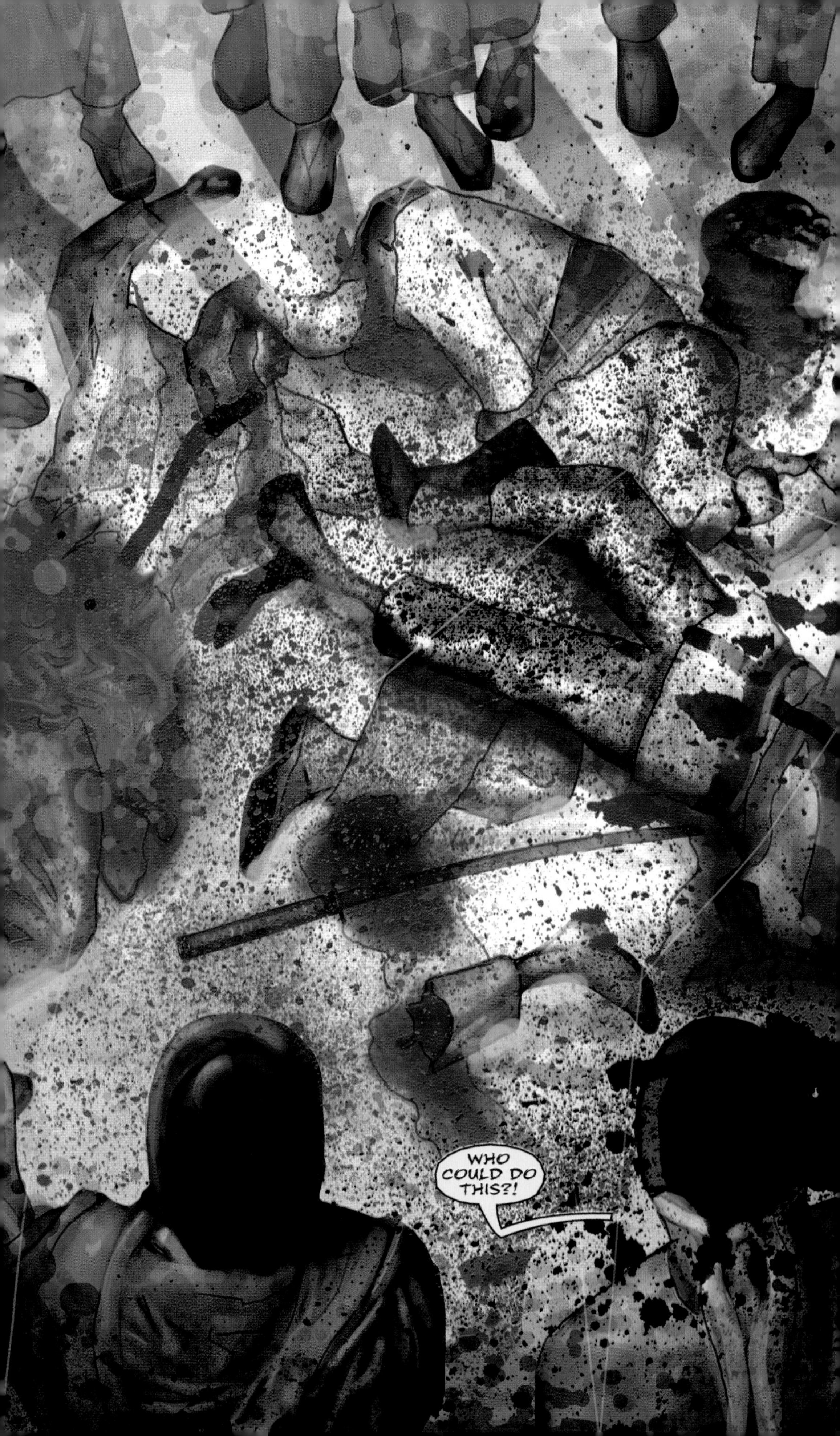
WHO COULD DO THIS?!

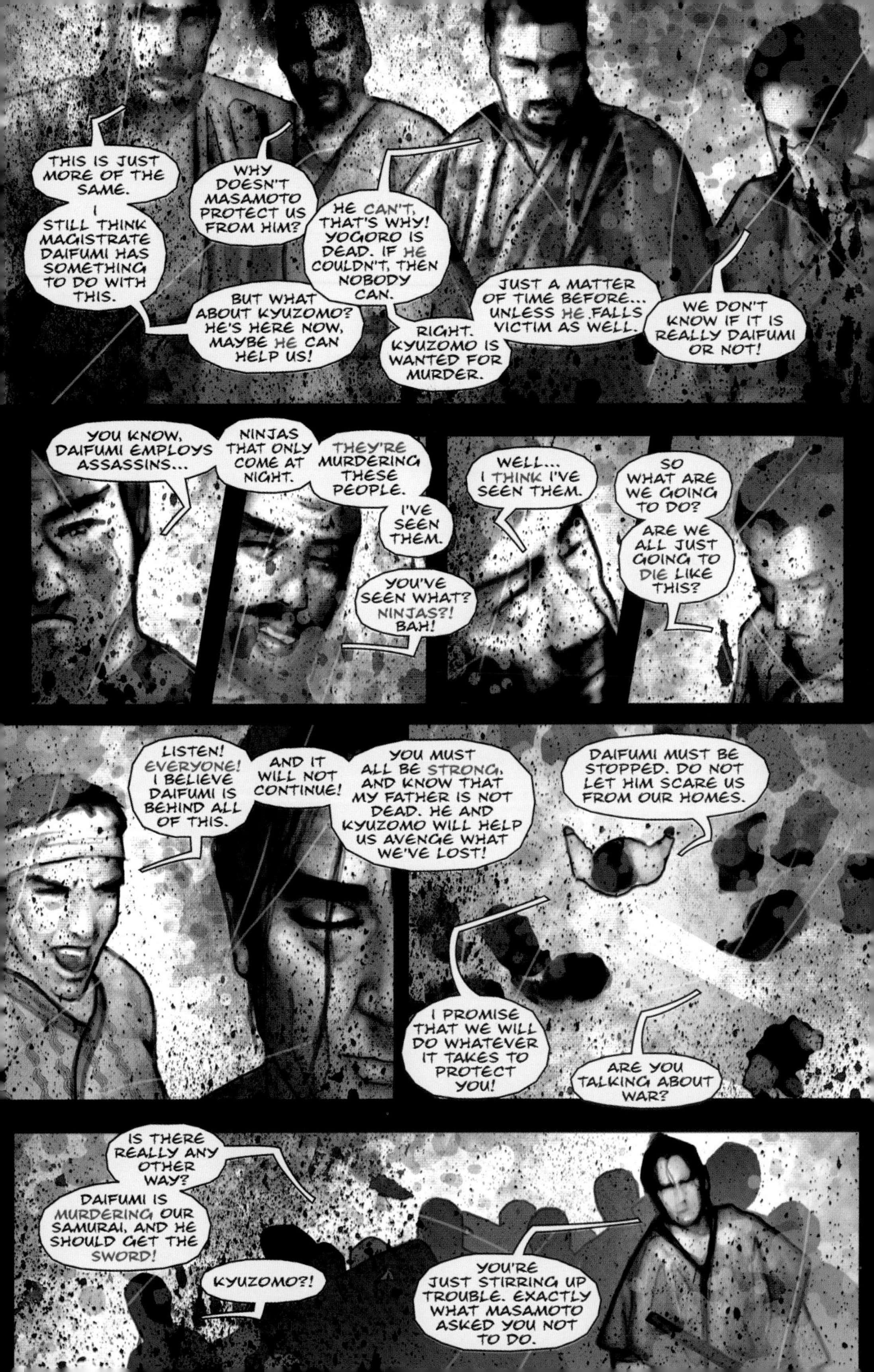

THIS IS JUST MORE OF THE SAME.
I STILL THINK MAGISTRATE DAIFUMI HAS SOMETHING TO DO WITH THIS.
WHY DOESN'T MASAMOTO PROTECT US FROM HIM?
HE CAN'T, THAT'S WHY! YOGORO IS DEAD. IF HE COULDN'T, THEN NOBODY CAN.
BUT WHAT ABOUT KYUZOMO? HE'S HERE NOW, MAYBE HE CAN HELP US!
RIGHT. KYUZOMO IS WANTED FOR MURDER.
JUST A MATTER OF TIME BEFORE... UNLESS HE FALLS VICTIM AS WELL.
WE DON'T KNOW IF IT IS REALLY DAIFUMI OR NOT!
YOU KNOW, DAIFUMI EMPLOYS ASSASSINS...
NINJAS THAT ONLY COME AT NIGHT.
THEY'RE MURDERING THESE PEOPLE.
I'VE SEEN THEM.
YOU'VE SEEN WHAT? NINJAS?! BAH!
WELL... I THINK I'VE SEEN THEM.
SO WHAT ARE WE GOING TO DO?
ARE WE ALL JUST GOING TO DIE LIKE THIS?
LISTEN! EVERYONE! I BELIEVE DAIFUMI IS BEHIND ALL OF THIS.
AND IT WILL NOT CONTINUE!
YOU MUST ALL BE STRONG, AND KNOW THAT MY FATHER IS NOT DEAD. HE AND KYUZOMO WILL HELP US AVENGE WHAT WE'VE LOST!
DAIFUMI MUST BE STOPPED. DO NOT LET HIM SCARE US FROM OUR HOMES.
I PROMISE THAT WE WILL DO WHATEVER IT TAKES TO PROTECT YOU!
ARE YOU TALKING ABOUT WAR?
IS THERE REALLY ANY OTHER WAY?
DAIFUMI IS MURDERING OUR SAMURAI, AND HE SHOULD GET THE SWORD!
KYUZOMO?!
YOU'RE JUST STIRRING UP TROUBLE. EXACTLY WHAT MASAMOTO ASKED YOU NOT TO DO.

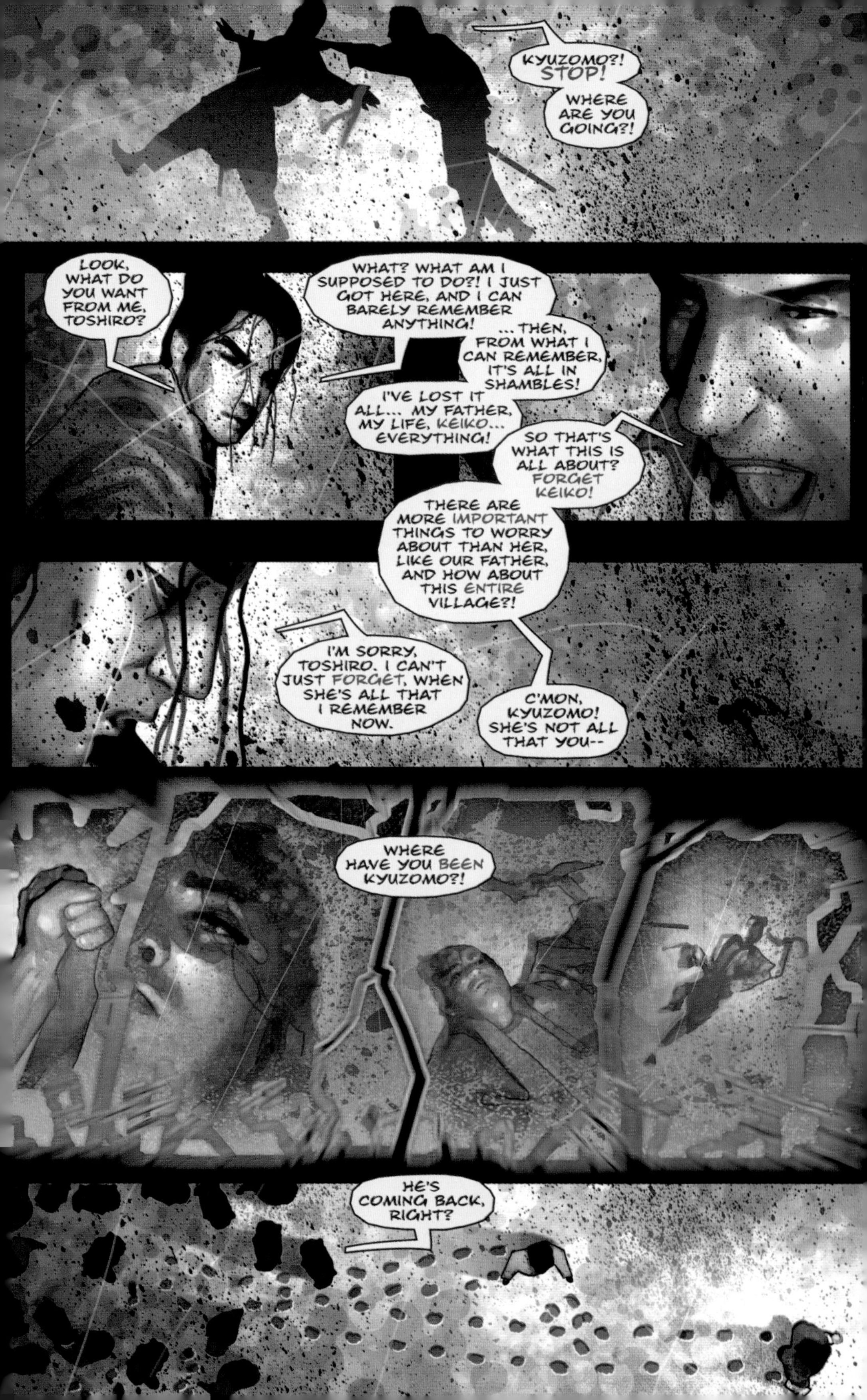
KYUZOMO?! STOP!
WHERE ARE YOU GOING?!
LOOK, WHAT DO YOU WANT FROM ME, TOSHIRO?
WHAT? WHAT AM I SUPPOSED TO DO?! I JUST GOT HERE, AND I CAN BARELY REMEMBER ANYTHING!
... THEN, FROM WHAT I CAN REMEMBER, IT'S ALL IN SHAMBLES!
I'VE LOST IT ALL... MY FATHER, MY LIFE, KEIKO... EVERYTHING!
SO THAT'S WHAT THIS IS ALL ABOUT? FORGET KEIKO!
THERE ARE MORE IMPORTANT THINGS TO WORRY ABOUT THAN HER, LIKE OUR FATHER, AND HOW ABOUT THIS ENTIRE VILLAGE?!
I'M SORRY, TOSHIRO. I CAN'T JUST FORGET, WHEN SHE'S ALL THAT I REMEMBER NOW.
C'MON, KYUZOMO! SHE'S NOT ALL THAT YOU--
WHERE HAVE YOU BEEN KYUZOMO?!
HE'S COMING BACK, RIGHT?

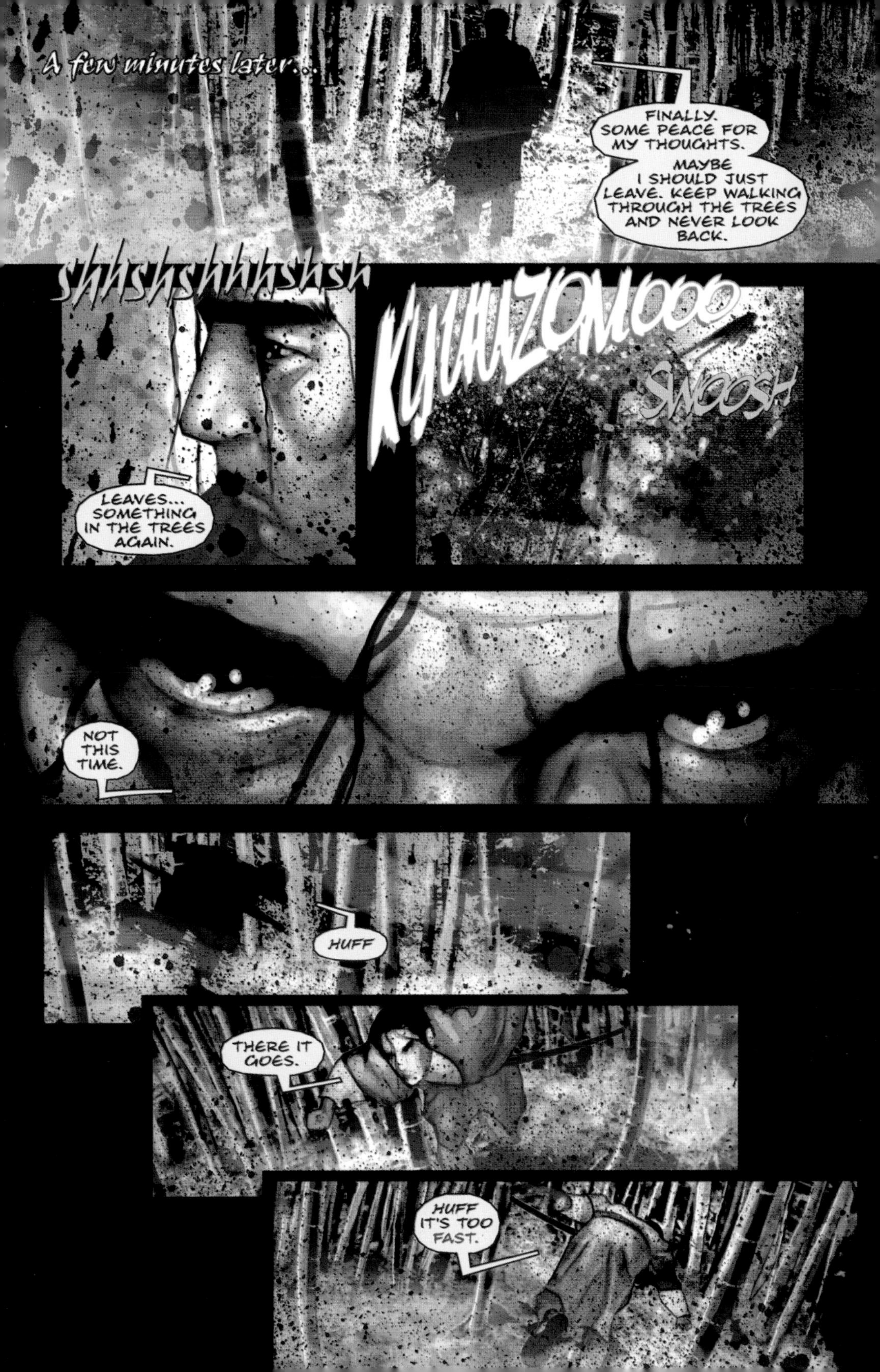
A few minutes later...
FINALLY. SOME PEACE FOR MY THOUGHTS.
MAYBE I SHOULD JUST LEAVE. KEEP WALKING THROUGH THE TREES AND NEVER LOOK BACK.
shhshshhhshsh
LEAVES... SOMETHING IN THE TREES AGAIN.
KYUHHZOMOOO
SWOOSH
NOT THIS TIME.
HUFF
THERE IT GOES.
HUFF IT'S TOO FAST.

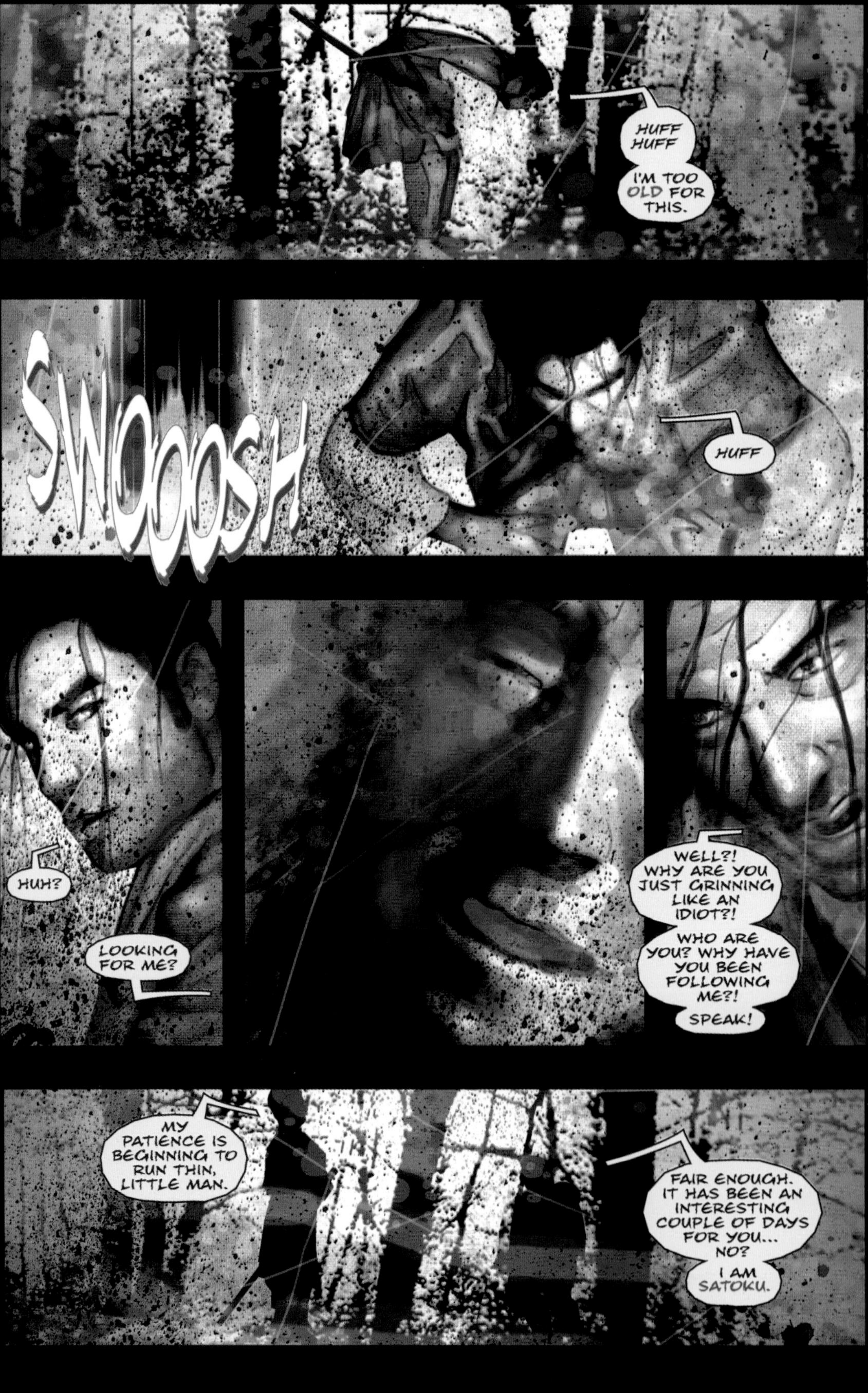
HUFF HUFF
I'M TOO OLD FOR THIS.
SWOOSH
HUFF
HUH?
LOOKING FOR ME?
WELL?! WHY ARE YOU JUST GRINNING LIKE AN IDIOT?!
WHO ARE YOU? WHY HAVE YOU BEEN FOLLOWING ME?!
SPEAK!
MY PATIENCE IS BEGINNING TO RUN THIN, LITTLE MAN.
FAIR ENOUGH. IT HAS BEEN AN INTERESTING COUPLE OF DAYS FOR YOU... NO?
I AM SATOKU.

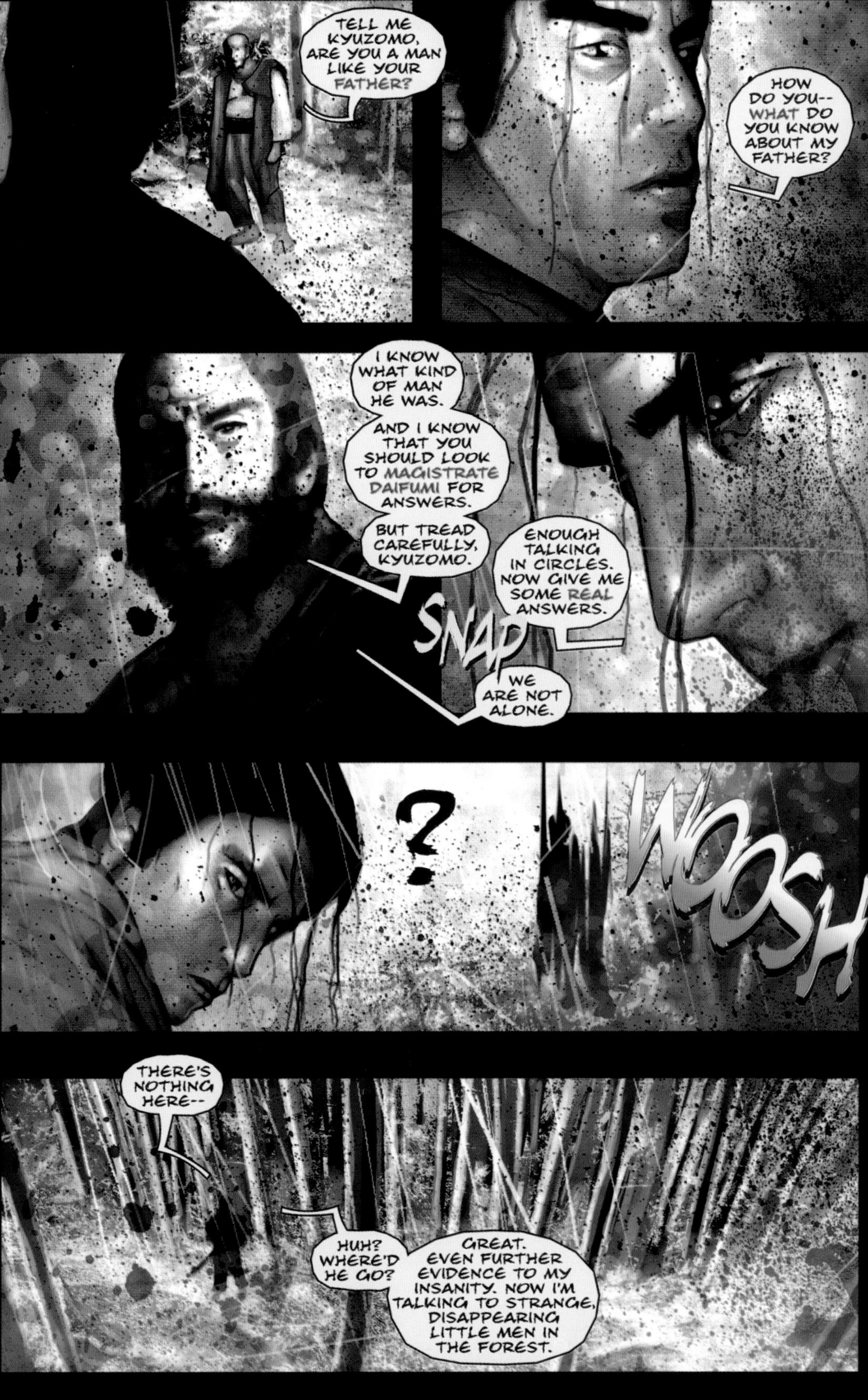
TELL ME KYUZOMO, ARE YOU A MAN LIKE YOUR FATHER?
HOW DO YOU-- WHAT DO YOU KNOW ABOUT MY FATHER?
I KNOW WHAT KIND OF MAN HE WAS.
AND I KNOW THAT YOU SHOULD LOOK TO MAGISTRATE DAIFUMI FOR ANSWERS.
BUT TREAD CAREFULLY, KYUZOMO.
ENOUGH TALKING IN CIRCLES. NOW GIVE ME SOME REAL ANSWERS.
SNAP
WE ARE NOT ALONE.
?
WOOSH
THERE'S NOTHING HERE--
HUH? WHERE'D HE GO?
GREAT. EVEN FURTHER EVIDENCE TO MY INSANITY. NOW I'M TALKING TO STRANGE, DISAPPEARING LITTLE MEN IN THE FOREST.

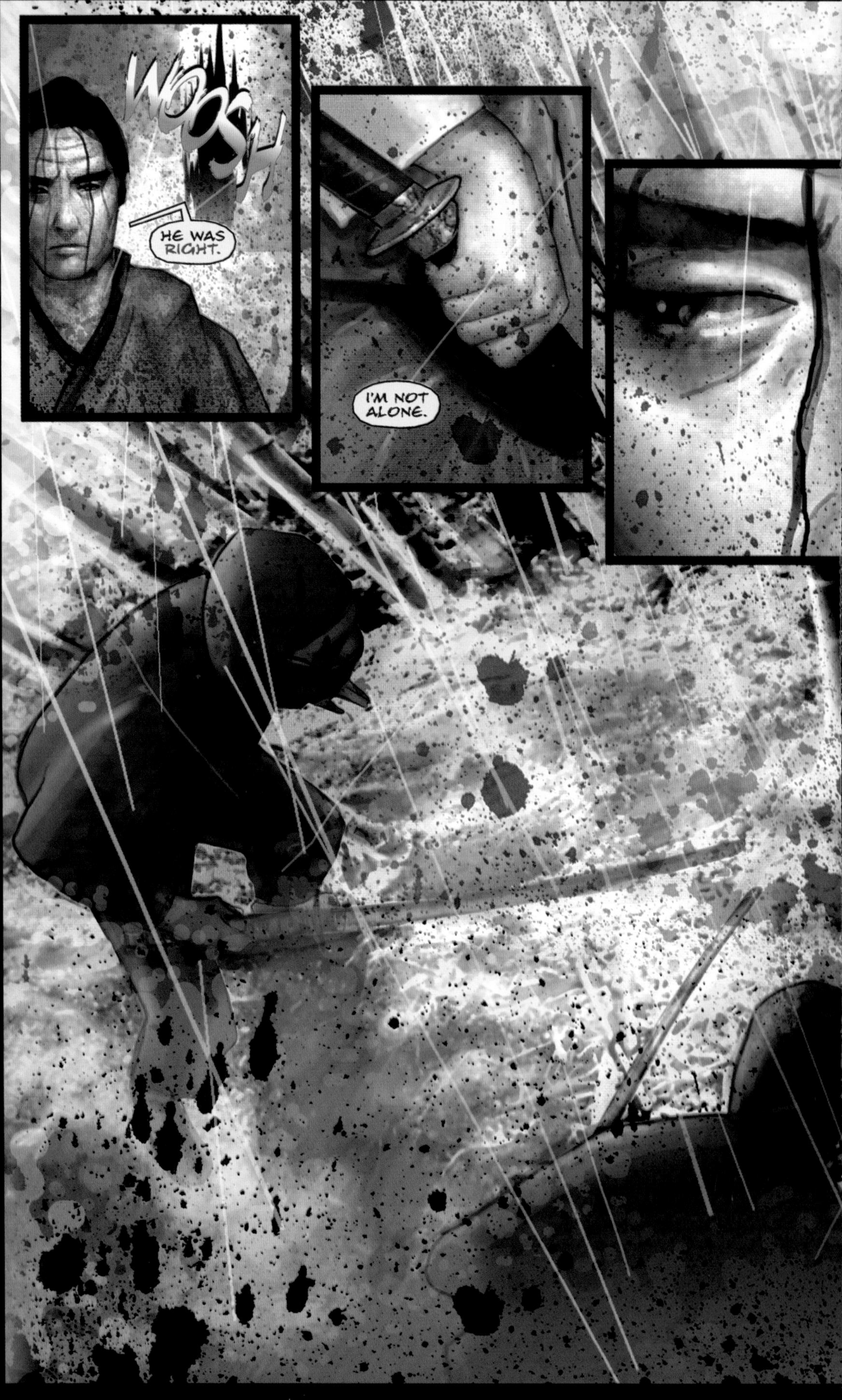
WOOSH
HE WAS RIGHT.
I'M NOT ALONE.

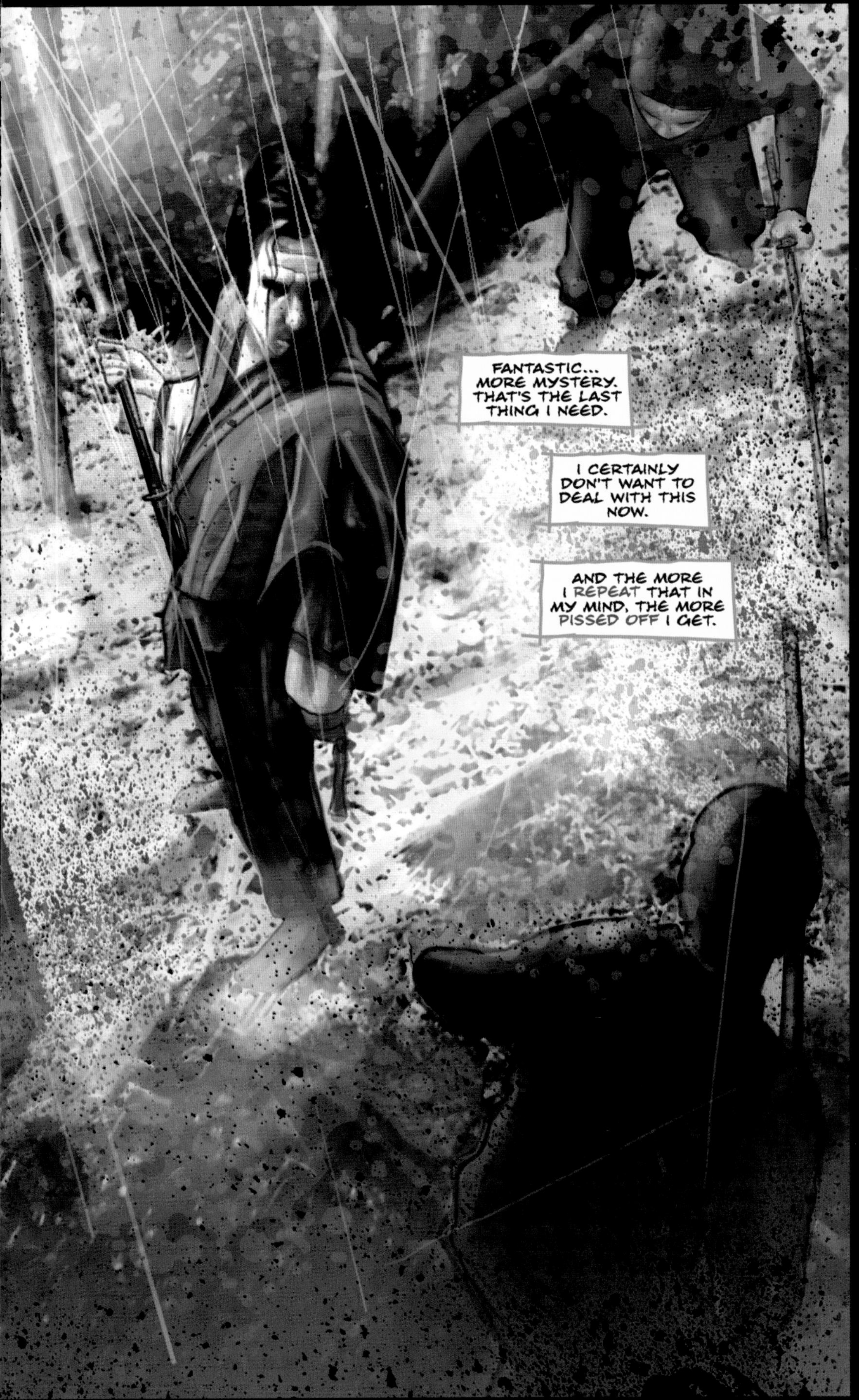
FANTASTIC... MORE MYSTERY. THAT'S THE LAST THING I NEED.
I CERTAINLY DON'T WANT TO DEAL WITH THIS NOW.
AND THE MORE I REPEAT THAT IN MY MIND, THE MORE PISSED OFF I GET.

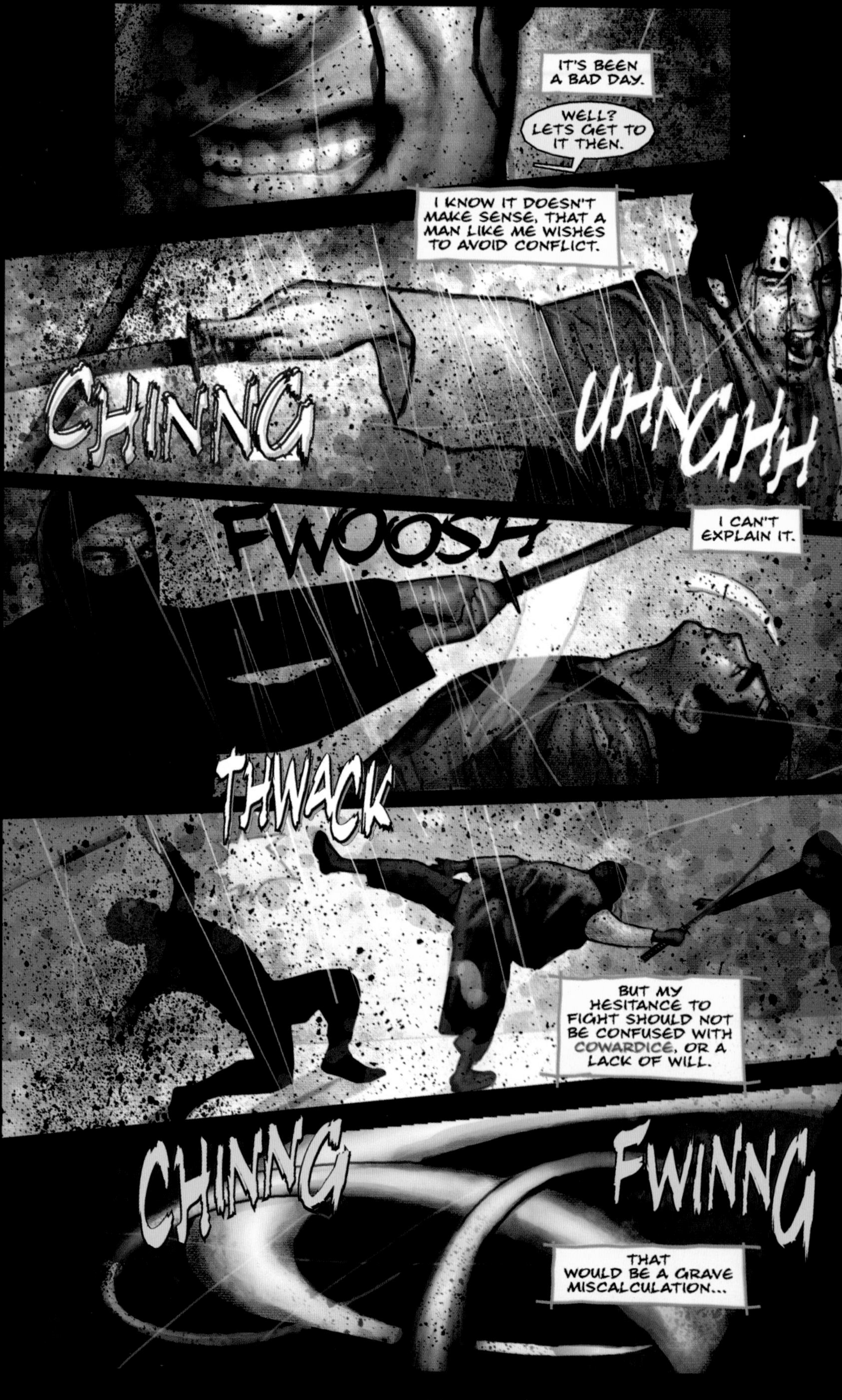
IT'S BEEN A BAD DAY.
WELL? LETS GET TO IT THEN.
I KNOW IT DOESN'T MAKE SENSE, THAT A MAN LIKE ME WISHES TO AVOID CONFLICT.
CHINNG
UHNGHH
FWOOSH
I CAN'T EXPLAIN IT.
THWACK
BUT MY HESITANCE TO FIGHT SHOULD NOT BE CONFUSED WITH COWARDICE, OR A LACK OF WILL.
CHINNG
FWINNG
THAT WOULD BE A GRAVE MISCALCULATION...

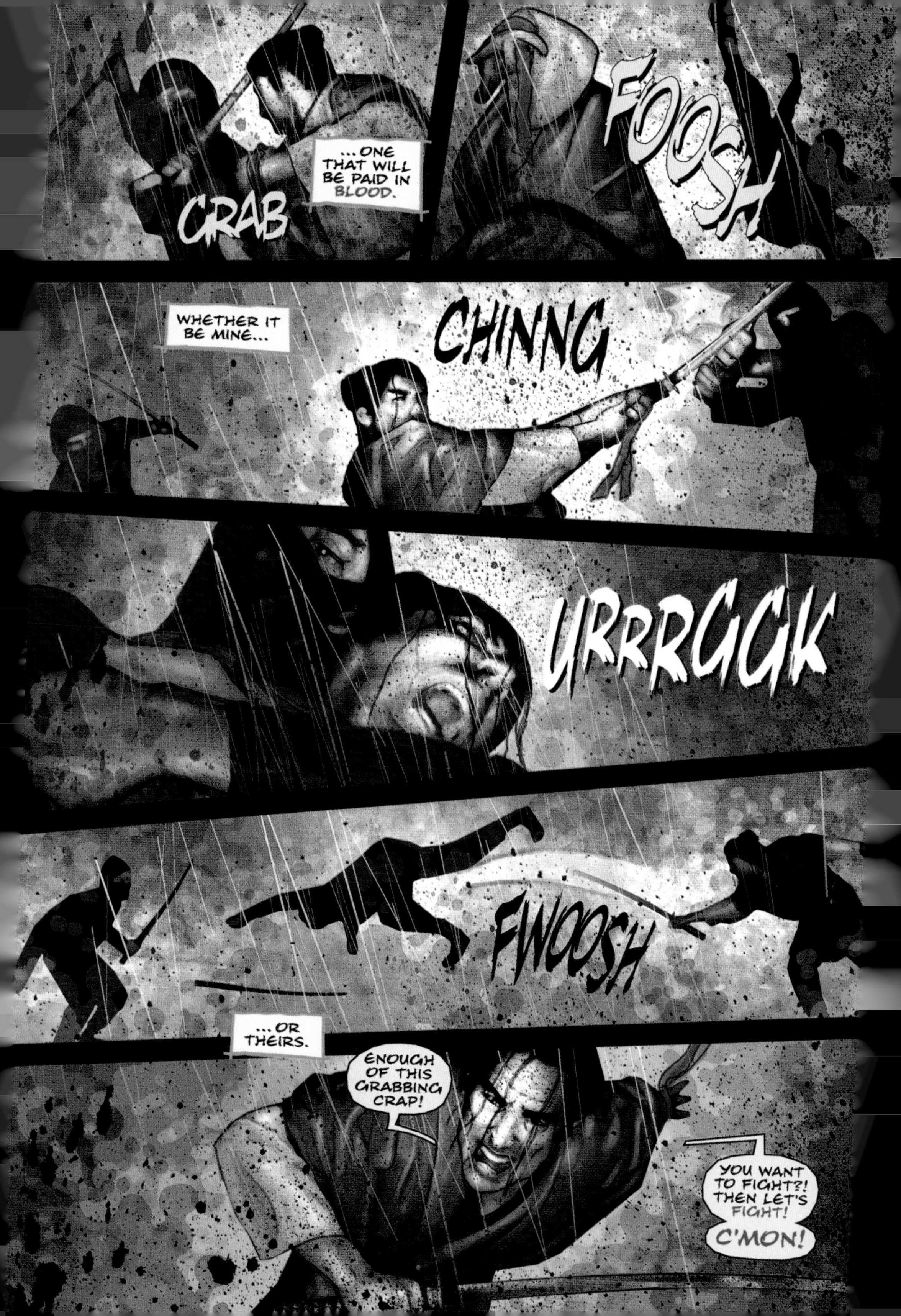
CRAB
...ONE THAT WILL BE PAID IN BLOOD.
FOOSH
WHETHER IT BE MINE...
CHINNG
URRRGGK
FWOOSH
...OR THEIRS.
ENOUGH OF THIS GRABBING CRAP!
YOU WANT TO FIGHT?! THEN LET'S FIGHT!
C'MON!

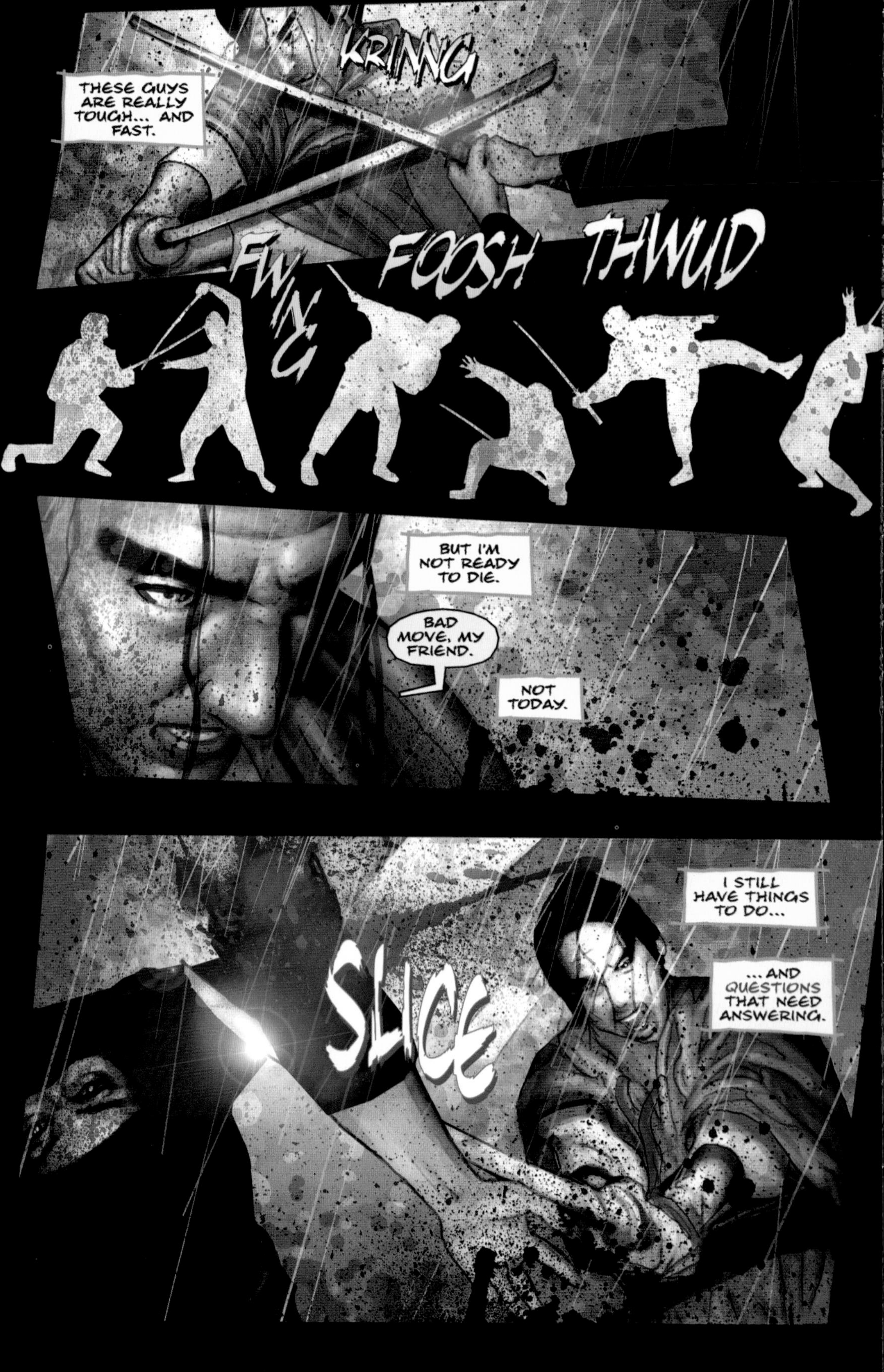

KRINNG
THESE GUYS ARE REALLY TOUGH... AND FAST.
FWING
FOOSH
THWUD
BUT I'M NOT READY TO DIE.
BAD MOVE, MY FRIEND.
NOT TODAY.
I STILL HAVE THINGS TO DO...
SLICE
...AND QUESTIONS THAT NEED ANSWERING.

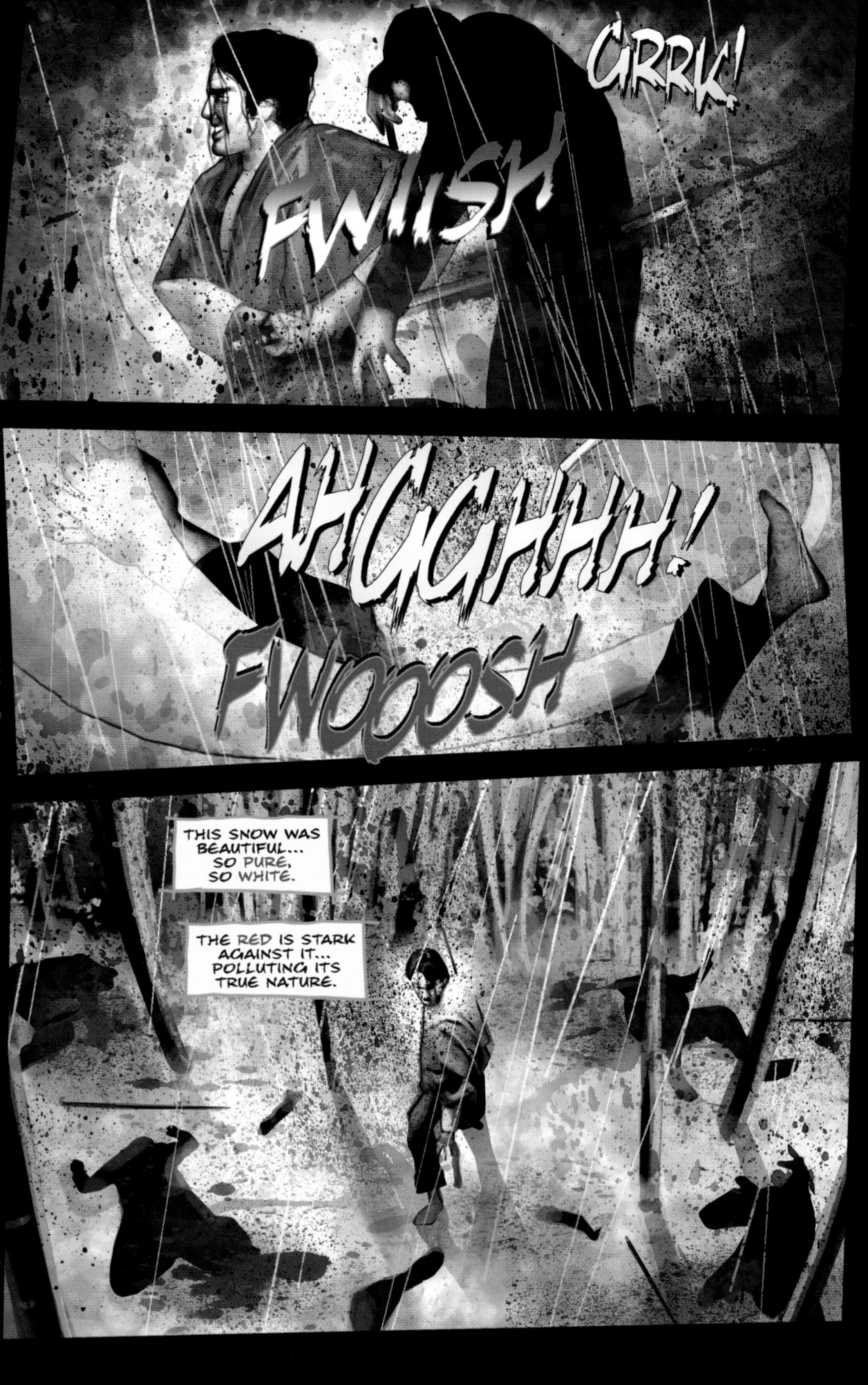
GRRK!
FWISH
AHGGHHH!
FWOOOSH
THIS SNOW WAS BEAUTIFUL... SO PURE, SO WHITE.
THE RED IS STARK AGAINST IT... POLLUTING ITS TRUE NATURE.

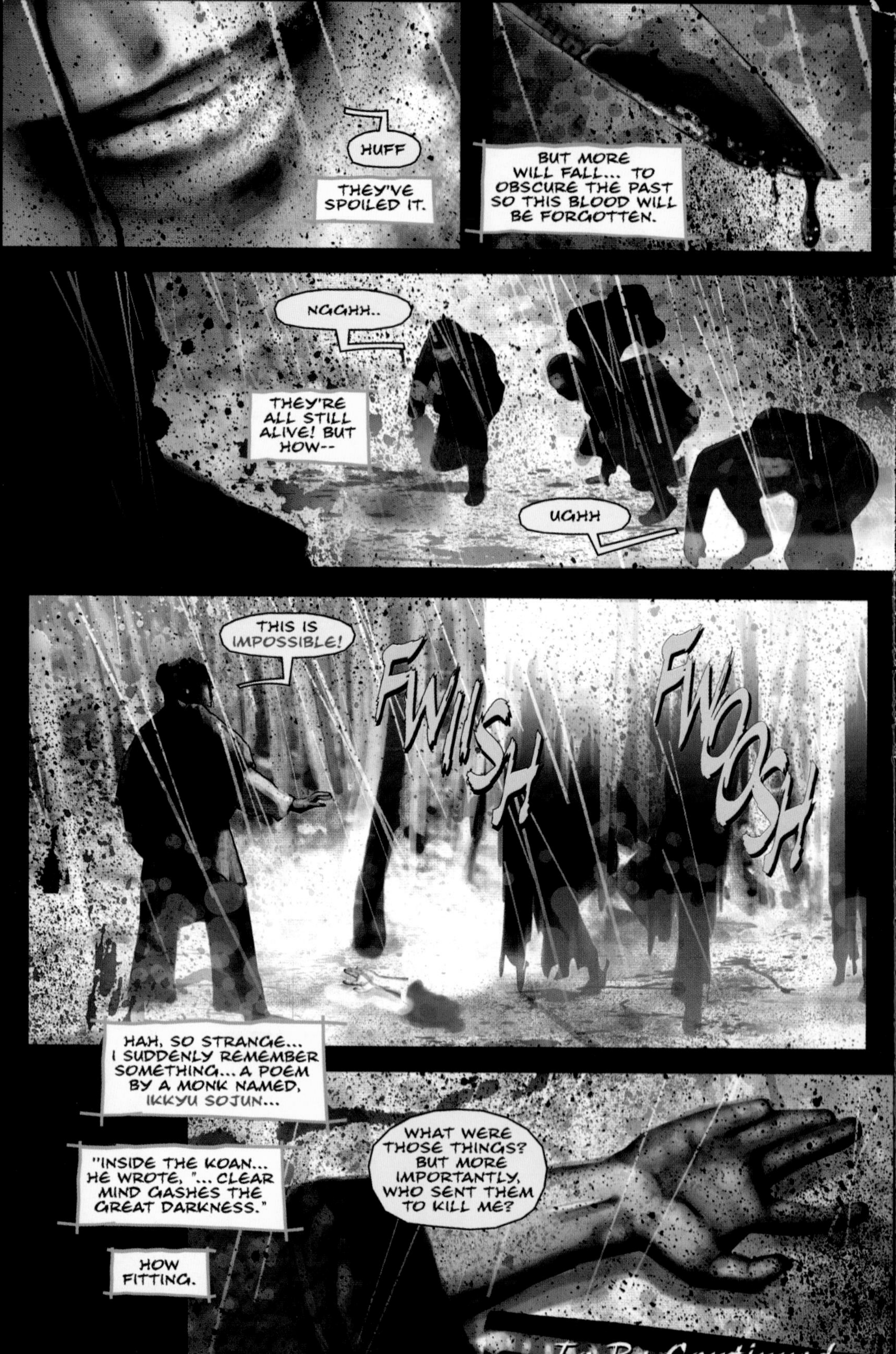
HUFF
THEY'VE SPOILED IT.
BUT MORE WILL FALL... TO OBSCURE THE PAST SO THIS BLOOD WILL BE FORGOTTEN.
NGGHH..
THEY'RE ALL STILL ALIVE! BUT HOW--
UGHH
THIS IS IMPOSSIBLE!
FWISH
FWOOSH
HAH, SO STRANGE... I SUDDENLY REMEMBER SOMETHING... A POEM BY A MONK NAMED, IKKYU SOJUN...
"INSIDE THE KOAN... HE WROTE, "... CLEAR MIND GASHES THE GREAT DARKNESS."
HOW FITTING.
WHAT WERE THOSE THINGS? BUT MORE IMPORTANTLY, WHO SENT THEM TO KILL ME?
To Be Continued...

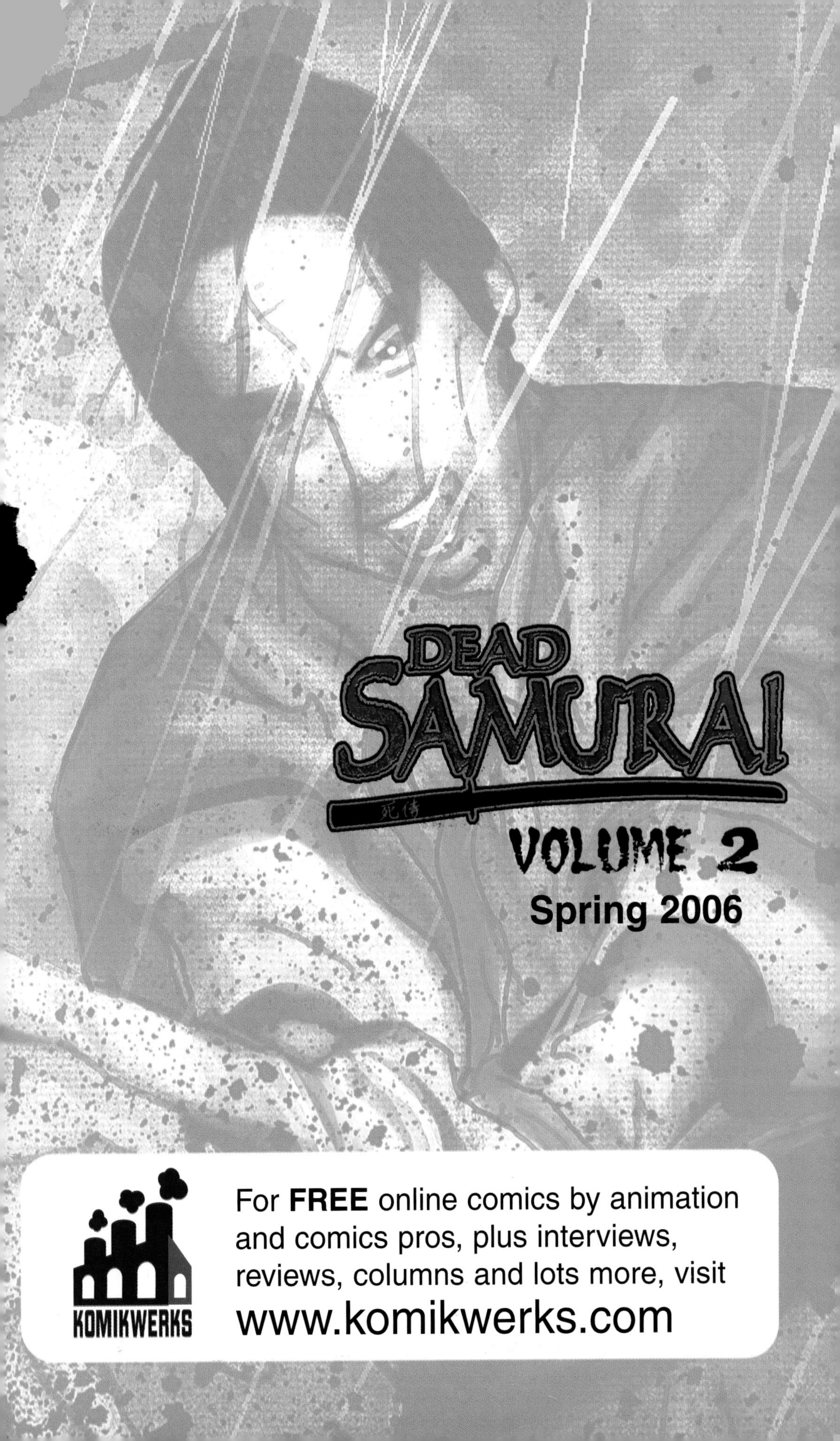
DEAD
SAMURAI
死侍
VOLUME 2
Spring 2006
For **FREE** online comics by animation and comics pros, plus interviews, reviews, columns and lots more, visit
www.komikwerks.com
KOMIKWERKS